Saturday Night at Magellan's

Stories

Charles Rafferty

Fomite
Burlington, VT

ISBN-13: 978-1-937677-53-4
Library of Congress Control Number: 2013941561

Fomite
58 Peru Street
Burlington, VT 05401
www.fomitepress.com

Cover photo - Wendy Rafferty

For Laurence McNamara

Contents

III.

Acknowledgments

Saturday Night at Magellan's — *Louisiana Literature*
Skywriting — *Tattoo Highway*
My Grandfather's Silver — *The Cortland Review*
Engagement — *The Pedestal*
Orchard Bright — *Sonora Review*
Conductor — *Staccato*
Europe Is the Invention of Americans — *Per Contra*
The Secret Thoughts of Thomas, the Clerk in Men's Wear
— *Atticus Review, Nanoism*
Coyote — *Superstition Review*
Rain — *Foliate Oak Literary Magazine*
The Ring — *The Fiddleback*
Too Beautiful — *Citron Review*
Excerpt of an Interview With a Man Threatening to Blow
Up His Local Branch — *A-Minor*
Practice — *A Clean, Well-Lighted Place*
Graffiti — *South85*
Dump — *The Drum Literary Magazine*
The Blanket — *Prick of the Spindle*
Stamina — *Sheepshead Review*
Stars — *Mary*
279 Waterloo Street — *Slab*
Death Comes to Parker Grove — *Bound Off*
I've Seen It in the Movies — *Atticus Review*
From Hammonton, New Jersey: The Land of Berries —
Temenos

Words — *Burrow Press*

Thief — *Burning Word*

An Incident at the Stamford Train Station — *Pembroke*

Modest Blouses and Flowing Skirts — *The Meadow*

Late — *Conium Review*

Dance Lesson — *Red Earth Review*

My Yoga Pants, My Executioner — *Flash Fiction Funny Anthology*

The Spill — *SpringGun*

The Man Waiting for the Light to Change — *SpringGun*

"Orchard Bright" was a finalist in the 2011 *Sonora Review* Fiction Contest.

I.

My Grandfather's Silver

When I was seven, my grandfather stubbed his cigar out in the upright ashtray he kept his hand on like a cane. He took a long sip from his afternoon highball, staring into my eyes until I felt like I should speak.

"I want to show you something," he said, cutting me off.

I followed him down the narrow cellar steps. When we got to the bottom, he pulled the chain to a light I could never reach, and took me over to a hole in the cinderblocks that led under the back bedroom. From this crawlspace, he pulled first a dust-covered tarp, and then a metal strongbox. I could tell by the way he braced the chair against the wall and cursed that it was the heaviest thing he'd picked up in years.

He put his finger to his mouth and spoke to me in a whisper. "When I'm dead, this box is yours. I want you to remember that. After the funeral, you come down here and you get this box."

Then he added, importantly: "Don't let anyone know you

have it." He pointed his thumb at the ceiling, where here and there the boards creaked with the weight of my mother and sisters.

He took a key from his pocket and popped the lock. Inside, it was full of the coins he'd been hoarding since when he first heard silver was getting phased out. The box held roll after roll of Mercury dimes and Franklin half-dollars. He even had a roll of wartime nickels — when they put in a little silver to make up for the nickel they needed for tanks and bullets.

We spent the next half-hour going through them. He showed me what was oldest and what was best. He showed me the pure, copperless look of the ridges when they were stacked into little towers. Afterward, my fingers smelled like metal.

"How come you're giving it to me?"

"You're the only collector in the family," he said. "I've seen your stash." He was referring to the bag of wheat pennies and the three buffalo nickels worn so smooth you could only tell it was an Indian for sure by the direction of the profile. "Everyone else'll cash this in. Silver is paying big money. Too much temptation for the rest of them." He put the key in my hand and told me to take care of it.

He still had a cigar going in the upright when he died three days later, and because his gift and my promise were still ringing in my ears, I went down to the basement when everyone was drunk and grieving, and somehow hauled that box upstairs and out the side door, where I hid it under the back seat of my mother's station wagon. It ended up at the bottom of my bureau drawer, covered with the sweaters I never wore. That's where it stayed for the next twelve years.

Now, for the second time this week, I'm pulling it out and opening a roll in search of a coppery edge. There aren't any of course. They're all Liberty quarters. And I am drunk and out of a job, and wanting a cigarette. In a moment, I'll take six of the quarters to the tavern across the street where they have a machine, and I can just imagine the cigarette man when he sees the silver quarters in the little stacks on his kitchen table. Maybe he puts it together — somebody's coin collection balanced against the wish for smoke. More likely it's just his lucky day, because he's got a bit of a collection himself, which he'd always wanted to give his grandson — the sensible one, the one who knows how to save.

***

COYOTE

On the way back from the hardware store, I see the coyote on the side of Route 84. It is big and wolfish and dead. Two crows stand beside him, looking for a place to begin.

Later that day, while I'm dropping off my daughter at a birthday party, the mothers are all talking about the dead coyote: "big as my father's shepherd," "like it was sleeping," "gray like our van," "a buzzard with a head up its ass."

It's a small town. Everyone worries about the coyotes they never see. Someone has told us they'll eat our pets, our three-year-olds. It doesn't matter that we know about odds, that no one has ever been killed by a coyote in this state. The coyote is our boogey-man. Now that we've seen him dead, our apprehension, oddly, increases: "they travel in packs," "the den must be close," "they get hungrier in winter, more desperate."

The party is one where the mothers are going to stay. And even though I'm just a father, I decide to stay too. I settle in to the iced tea and gossip. I help police the dozen roving daughters as the woman from Critter Fun comes in with her hedgehogs and snakes to delight us all. None of the animals, no matter how strange, make us recoil. Even the giant cockroaches are passed around and petted.

I tell the mothers I saw the coyote too, earlier, maybe just after it happened. They nod and sip their drinks, waiting for their chance to touch the airy warmth of the chinchilla — so light in your lap you could forget it was even there.

By the end of the party, my daughter is cranky with cake and her first real soda. She has to be forcibly strapped into the car. I take the long way home on 84 to make her fall asleep, figuring I can show her the coyote if she's still awake. But the coyote is gone when I get there. Not a trace. Could it have been eaten that efficiently? Is there a taxidermist living among us? What if it was somebody's shepherd? Maybe it *was* just sleeping?

My daughter is unconscious in the rearview mirror, and the woods along the highway are getting dark. I get off at the next exit and follow the road to our house — taking the route that everyone knows. We pass the animal hospital, the streetlight with a bluish tint, the low stone wall that keeps out nothing, and the oak on the outer curve with seventeen reflectors nailed into its bark to tell the world beware.

These are the landmarks we give to friends, drifting by like breadcrumbs that anything could follow.

***

Death Comes to Parker Grove

Everyone at the barbecue is talking about it — the death of Karin, the woman who lived on the next street over. Her daughter, Melissa, is the friend of all of our daughters, though none of us knew the parents well. It's too soon for an obituary, so we're all theorizing, guessing our way into the grave with her.

"I think she killed herself," says Joyce. Joyce is the woman who likes to be known as the person who said an unpleasant thing first.

"I thought she had cancer," says Mike.

"I saw her pushing a shopping cart full of kids in the Big Y last week. Cancer wasn't her problem," says Joyce.

I take a fork and jab it into the kielbasa bursting apart on a grill so old I can't keep the flame even. I drag it onto a plate and look for the mustard.

"We were supposed to have Melissa over this weekend," says Tonya. "I don't know what to tell Kristina. She's never had anyone she knows die before."

"Tell her that god likes killing good people," says Joyce. Joyce is an atheist. She likes to remind people that when god got mad at the pharaoh, he started killing the babies of Egypt.

"Don't say that," says Tonya. "You're going to bring something down on yourself. You're going to make it so you're sorry." Tonya goes to church every Sunday. She's a Presbyterian. The day after Thanksgiving, she hangs an angel on her door.

"I thought you thought she killed herself," says Mike. He was looking off at the trees around the yard as if he might have heard someone calling for him.

I can tell Joyce is weighing out whether she wants to fight with both Mike and Tonya, or to just let it lie. She looks up into the sky — perfectly blue and doilied with August-still maples — and shakes her head. It looks like she's chiding a small child who happens to be a god who isn't really there.

"Same difference," she says.

Everybody takes an extra sip from their beer or, in Joyce's case, her vodka and lime. We're all in our forties. So was Karin. The faithful and the faithless are all more shaken than we expected at the death of a woman we barely knew.

I start passing around the kielbasa. The toothpicks are topped with little clouds of cellophane.

"They look like tufts of colored pubic hair," says Joyce, popping one into her mouth.

Everyone stabs a disk of meat as the plate goes around. I look across the lawn to where my own daughter is swinging on a vine, the other kids waiting their turn. "Don't swing out so far," I yell. It's the warning I always give.

The vine swings over a hill. The farther you swing, the farther your fall. If that old grape vine broke at the right moment, my daughter would snap an ankle, maybe a shin. But I've swung that vine myself, and it never gives.

"She killed herself, sure as shit," says Joyce. "She knew what was coming and she pulled the rug right out from under it. She did the right thing."

"Either way, it was cancer," says Mike. He says it with authority, reaching his toothpick for another kielbasa.

Beyond my swinging daughter, through the humid air, amid the oaks and maples and cherry trees, I see the roof of Melissa's house, its curtained windows, the smokeless chimney. I imagine the rooms milling with grief and cousins. I push a piece of kielbasa into my mouth. The mustard is hot and good. My daughter pushes farther out on her tremulous dying vine. There are other vines, still connected and alive, and reaching up into the woods around us. If there are grapes, they're too high up to see, harvested by birds with black and perilous wings.

***

Skywriting

The sky above the highway was blue, and the wind was scudding among a few bright clouds. Davis and Laura were returning from a funeral where the first rifle report had made her gasp.

Laura had wanted to go to the luncheon afterward, but Davis said they should go straight home. "I have to cut the lawn. Tomorrow's supposed to rain," he said.

"I feel like I should say something to his mother, his other friends," said Laura.

"Come on," he said. "We'll never see these people again."

This was true. Laura had only known Jimmy for a little while. He was a salesman in the office below hers. She met him because their afternoon cigarette breaks overlapped. They complained about paperwork and what you couldn't expense. Then, on Monday, someone from the other office saw her smoking alone and came out to tell her that Jimmy had died in his car.

So they left directly from the cemetery. Laura flipped through the stations trying to find a decent song. Before she could settle on something, they entered the West Rock Tunnel, and the radio gradually disappeared. They said nothing in the tunnel. They never did. Davis was superstitious and believed the mountain would fall on them. Laura didn't think so, of course, but she knew he would not answer if she chose to speak to him in the dark and hum of the tunnel. When they burst into sunlight on the other side, the radio was full of harpsichord.

"Skywriters!" said Laura as she leaned forward and pointed at the air above Davis's shoulder.

High above them, five black specks were leaving their message in a dot-matrix fashion. At first, the letters were crisp and perfectly spaced, but they quickly blurred, as though the writing were in a painting by Renoir. They were spelling out something about the Mohegan Sun casino, but by the time the last "n" had been completed, the beginning of the phrase had turned to ordinary cloud.

"Not the best day for it," said Davis. "They should all fly home."

"It's supposed to go away," said Laura, watching the letters emerge and blur and keep on coming. "It's for the people headed east. They'd eventually piece it together."

Davis could see this was probably true. The line of writ-

ing stretched less and less legibly into the west, as if someone had half-heartedly erased a blackboard.

Laura didn't like harpsichords, though she couldn't
say why, and all the stations in range had gone to com-
mercials, so she turned the radio off. She craned her neck
to see what the skywriters were doing, now behind her.
Something about "Sunday" was all she could make out,
and then the highway curved north and the skywriters
were gone for good.

"You know, a boy wrote something in the sky for me
once," she said.

Davis affected nonchalance. "Billy?" he asked.

Billy was the love of Laura's life long before she'd known
Davis. Billy was the high school sweetheart, and he'd never
left the town they grew up in. At least Laura assumed he
was still there. The summer before she left South Jersey for
Vanderbilt, Billy had arranged a picnic in one of the fallow
meadows of his father's soybean farm. They ate triangular
sandwiches and drank a bottle of red wine that Billy had
gotten from his older cousin. He kept checking his watch
and scanning the sky. At the appointed time, Billy stopped
kissing her and told her to look up — and as if by magic a
heart was drawn on the horizon in front of them.

"That's for you," Billy said. He explained he didn't have
enough money for words. Then he leaned back, dug a cam-

era out of the basket, and snapped her picture with the heart beside her in the air, like a companion.

"It sounds like he wanted to marry you or something," said Davis.

"I think he did," said Laura. She said this looking from her lap to her own window.

The conversation suddenly felt dangerous for both of them. "How do you know?"

"He was just sweet," she said, trying to see the house on the hill she always wondered about when they drove this part of the highway. "But he never actually asked. I think he felt like he wasn't good enough."

"He wasn't," said Davis, trying to lighten the mood. He glanced over at Laura, but she was still at the window, watching the sun hit the glass of the fancy house. He looked back at the road and adjusted his hands on the wheel. "Why do you say that?"

"He never went to college. He just wanted to grow soybeans and settle down." She reached out and flipped the radio back on. "He knew I had other plans."

Davis let this sink in, imagining the pathetic hick Billy must have been and wondering how he could have such a hold on his wife, even now. She had studied architecture. She knew about wine. She read *The New Yorker*. She had an aversion to dirt and digging.

"Do you still have the picture?"

She told him she didn't, but this was a lie, and they spent the rest of the ride home listening to an Eighties Weekend that was back in progress.

*

Davis changed out of his suit, grabbed a beer, and went straight to the shed. He had a riding mower and a small lawn. Laura thought this made him look foolish as he backed up slowly and K-turned all over the tiny yard. It would be quicker with a push mower, but Davis was the kind of person who had to have things that his neighbors did not. It was a John Deere, the classic green. He looked like someone playing the part of a farmer.

Laura watched him now and then from the various windows of their home as she wandered among its rooms, wine in hand, putting away the laundry and sweeping up the dust. Eventually, she saw him back over and turn to mulch the azalea he had put in the ground for her last weekend. "Son of a bitch," she said as his head whipped around to the kitchen window to see if she had seen. But she was in the bedroom at the time, and his eye didn't wander that far.

*

Laura refilled her wineglass and went down to the basement. To Davis, it seemed like an impossible maze of bins and labeled boxes, but Laura had a knack for finding things down there. Davis had long ago ceded it to her. He preferred a beer in the gasoline smell of the shed — among the bags of lime and rat killer, the half-dozen cans of old paint that likely had hardened to the point of unusability.

Laura picked up a bin that held a mismatched pewter tea service she was saving in case they ever had a daughter. She put it on the floor by the furnace with a clank. Then she moved a bin labeled "Sweaters for Davis" on top of that. And then she pulled out the leather valise she used to carry in college. Her father had bought it for her so she could keep her life in order. "A good businesswoman knows where everything is," he had said. And for four years, the accordion dividers kept her courses in order. She never threw anything out until her grades showed up in the mail. Once, she had the paper that proved her grade in European Street Facades should in fact have been an A-, not a C. The professor apologized when she showed him the paper he had graded but forgotten to record.

Nowadays, Laura used the valise for keepsakes: old love letters from Davis, part of her prom corsage, a poem from one of the many silly boys she'd known before meeting Davis near the end of their senior year at college. A bandana, ticket stubs, a cork from the wine when she'd first slept over at a boy's apartment. It resembled what hides in the cushions of a couch in a very messy house. But Laura knew what each thing was and what each thing meant.

The photo of the heart was there as well. She picked it up and stared into it stonily, as if she were at a funeral among strangers. In the picture, she was young and smiling, and a portion of Billy's hand was in the frame from when he'd waved her into place. She felt what was happening and told herself to stop.

*

Davis found her in the bed, the blinds drawn, her back to him, the wineglass empty on the bedside table. He got a shower, and after he dressed, Laura was in the same position, the blinds a little bit darker. Now that he had gotten what he wanted, he began to wish they had gone to the luncheon. Why did he always deny his wife the thing that she wanted? He suspected that Laura was only pretending to sleep, that she was angry, but he didn't see what he could say to make her look at him with anything other than contempt.

He walked down the hall into the kitchen and poked around for something to eat, eventually heating up some leftovers — chicken and asparagus. He watched the plate turn inside the microwave and saw the fat clarify, drip, and collect. He wolfed it down and listened for some sign of movement from the bedroom: the turning of a page, the pushing and pulling of drawers, the creak of the bed as she got out of it. There wasn't anything, and the crack of the opened door was black with the night that was then arriving. So Davis poured himself a tumbler of bourbon, added a splash of cold water from the tap, and stepped onto the back porch.

*

It was dark enough for the first stars now. The wind that had blurred the skywriters was still blowing stiffly from the south. The tropical storm that had been promised for tomorrow seemed destined to arrive on schedule. High above him, the jets that were always there paced slowly across the sky. Their contrails fell apart and expanded in the moonlight coming over the trees. He could see the earlier contrails up there too. They looked like ordinary clouds now, but there was a vague straightness that gave them away, like someone had taken a broom to many trails of footsteps in the sand.

Davis heard something in the house. He downed his drink and went inside. The bedroom door was shut now, all the way. It was a crucial moment. The right gesture could stop this argument, or whatever it was. They could curl up together on the couch for a movie. But Davis could not say what that gesture should be. If someone put a gun to his head, he would have to guess, and the guess would be wild, as Laura knew. The closing of the door had said as much.

So Davis said nothing. He sat at the table as if a mountain of rock floated over him, awaiting the small vibration of his voice to call it down, to trap him there in that tunnel of dying air.

***

Too Beautiful

Men would pass her in the supermarket and change direction. They followed her — stopping when she stopped, loi-
tering in her bergamot wake, feeling for warmth on the cab-
bage she had touched. It lasted for aisles. Then, they checked
out, went home to their wives. Her life had been a series of
men deciding they should settle.

***

GRAFFITI

He's on his way to pick up a new handle for the storm door. It's been broken for weeks, and now that the season has changed, the cold is getting in. There's always a bunch of graffiti between his house and the hardware store — inscrutable lines and symbols that must mean something to somebody. So identical, they seem almost stenciled. But they're usually cursive, their size adapted to the available surface.

Graffiti didn't look like this when he was young. Its message was clear. He used to think "graffiti" was singular. He used to think you couldn't use a marker for this kind of thing. He used to think it would last forever, like hieroglyphics or the handprint silhouettes from that cave in France. But the city beautification projects turn the bridge trestles and highway pillars into a uniform gray. It's a thick industrial shade. Nothing leaks through. It creates a clean canvas for whoever is stupid enough to risk it.

He remembers his own stupidity, how he climbed down

from the woods above with an extension cord tied around his waist to spray paint in lemon letters that "Greer Davies is a goddess." The night cars of summer sped by on Route 91. It was virgin stone at the time. He had to write part of it while he was upside down. He had to rely on the only knot he knew to keep him tethered to the oak. He had to shrug it off when the whiskey slipped out of his pocket to the rocks forty feet below.

The next day, he drove Greer down the highway so she could see. Then he showed her the paint on his hands and shirt as a proof — a fine stippling of golden freckles. It was a gesture that let her say yes.

But in thirty years, a lot of idiots have had the same idea. In winter when the leaves are down, he can see a yellow "G" and part of a yellow "s." The rest is obscured by a mediocre Rolling Stones tongue, by "Mark Loves Tina," by "Dickhead Joe," by "Angelo 96."

Greer still comes back now and then to visit her folks for the holidays. He saw her stopped at a traffic light once, singing along to whatever was on the radio. She didn't turn when he beeped, and she and her music floated away when the traffic began again.

When he gets to the hardware store, he learns that the handle has been discontinued, that he'll have to replace the whole damn door, which is more than he expected.

He gets in the car and starts off down 91, headed for the rocks he'd painted with such clarity. The birches on the surrounding hills are a fumble of bones, and the air outside would turn his breath to fog if ever he tried to scale this stone to the height that he had been.

***

Dump

The car was full of the week's trash — the half-dozen bags through which the garbage was still discernible, the newspapers stacked on the back seat. He pulled out of the driveway and waved. He knew that his older daughter was watching him from one of the windows of their house, though he wasn't sure from which.

She was ten, and he had put her in charge of her seven-year-old sister. Their mother, he had heard, had done this once or twice — installing the older one in command for the duration of some small errand. But he, their father, had never done it. They'd always come to the dump with him as a kind of weekly field trip. Today they refused.

"It's too cold," they said. "Let us stay here." The television was full of cartoons. They had a Lego castle in progress on the dining room table. Outside, it was January — blue sky and ice for as far as he could see.

The rules were gone over — no opening the door, no answering the phone, no cooking with the gas stove, no drinking juice on the couch, no giving your sister medicine. It was a short list that he'd intended to be absolute, but the older daughter found an exception to every rule. "Yes," he said, "if the house is on fire, you can leave." "Yes," he said, "you can answer the phone if it's your grandmother." "Yes," he said, "if my car broke down and your sister had a fever, you could give her the Tylenol — the chewable tablets, children's strength. Be sure to read the label."

It was icier than he expected. If he died in some ditch, he wondered how long it would take before his children unbolted the dead-lock, before they believed the police that pounded on the door to tell them their fears were true, before they ventured onto the porch of their parentless world.

He made it back alive, and his daughters didn't look away from their cartoons. They had spent the last hour flipping the channels and pouring an extra large glass of juice apiece. They drank them on the couch despite his prohibitions. And when one of them spilled the juice, they just turned over the cushion.

This is what he found weeks later when he was vacuuming out the couch for the first time since his wife had left them — the pennies and popcorn rattling away. His daughters claimed not to remember how it got there, and this he decided was true enough for a world where people can stop coming home — sometimes without explanation, sometimes with so many they can't be held, like wild birds thrashing the air of a room they can't escape.

***

Practice

His eyes were lousy. Even when he remembered his glasses, he had a hard time seeing anything further than a book. Nevertheless, he knew his daughter was down there on the soccer field — running around on the perfect green of the synthetic grass. The twilight was coming on, and the giant lights had just buzzed to life. They were harsh, smothered already in swirling moths.

When he had parked the car, his daughter descended the hundred steps to the basin of the field without a word. They had been fighting. She wanted to go to a party with her friends. It was a night party. He had said no.

On the field, they were all 12-year-old girls with the same brown ponytail, the same blue uniform, the same ferocity. If he had to guess, his daughter would be that one charging the ball at midfield, the one who had yet to look in his direction.

Until these fights began, he had felt young. Now he felt as

his father must have felt, like every father when his presence becomes, palpably, something to be endured.

The color drained out of the western clouds. The field lights dominated. There were no stars. Even the twinkling of jetliners disappeared in the artificial glare, though he could hear their soft rumbling high above him as they passed.

The other fathers at the practice shouted advice from the bleachers. He had never been one of them. He believed that his daughter held this against him, that she saw it as evidence of her own incompetence, his lack of interest. It didn't matter that he drove to every practice, every game, that it was he who pushed her to join this band of girls who liked nothing more than to kick balls into oblivion.

"Good effort, Pam!" one of the fathers shouted. "Way to take it down the field, Jillian!" went another one. These fathers didn't yell about mistakes, only effort and success. His own silence shamed him.

The girl who was probably his daughter did something tricky with her feet, moving the ball between two defenders. It was beautiful, even from his blurry height. Given the right circumstances, such skill would always prevail. He knew that.

His daughter often said that he didn't see things correctly, that he couldn't understand what it was like to be her. She wondered why he couldn't see how pointless it was to hold her back when the rest of the world was rushing forward.

The last whistle blew, and he watched the girls gather up their sweatshirts and water bottles. One of them was heading for the steps below him. She still hadn't looked up, but he knew this was his daughter — returning to him like a duty. She charged the steps, determined to make him see that she was not tired, that she intended to pick back up whatever he hoped was dropped.

***

Conductor

As a joke, the conductor walked down the aisle of the 5:16 train saying "naked pictures, naked pictures" instead of "tickets, tickets" because there was a beautiful girl in the seat to his left.

The girl was not offended. She even pantomimed the motion of reaching into her purse for naked pictures.

Nevertheless, the conductor was beaten up. The girl's father happened to be in the seat behind her. She was 17, we learned.

We watched as she stamped her foot and yelled "Daddy," as her father wiped his bloody knuckles on the back of the conductor's shirt and pushed him off dazed in the other direction. The whole thing took six, maybe seven seconds.

We could tell the father was sorry to have to do it. Afterward, he stared into his lap. He said "not here" and "not now" in an even voice as his daughter questioned him, who said loudly that she didn't see the point.

The conductor, we knew, had daughters of his own, but they were still in the tea party phase. He could tell their future more clearly now and understood the necessity of this gesture in front of the daughter, that all of this was meant to keep the girl within the sphere of the father's influence for another year or two at best, a handful of days at worst. This is why he wouldn't press charges. This is why he waved off his fellow conductor when he lunged up the aisle to help. The bleeding man backed off to nurse his nose in a different car.

But the rest of us had to endure the father — his silent refusal to discuss anything in this forum, the daughter in a huff and pulling her sweatshirt close, the stockbroker beside her crammed up against the window as far as he could get.

And then the return to our newspapers and beers, the napping we intended. Until the daughter calmed down and began raking her nails through the auburn cloud of her hair and using her compact to fix her mascara — each of us drawn to that cyclopsian eye, afraid that it would catch us.

All of us, the men anyway, feared we'd find out what it was like to be beaten on a train — for not understanding the problem of daughters in a world full of people like us.

***

An Incident at the Stamford Train Station

I see a woman I know on the opposite platform whom I have not seen in years, but this crowd of people pressing into me prevents me from calling out. I don't want them to overhear my life, even my past life. And what if she doesn't recognize me after all these years, and I am left to look like one of those crazy train platform people who shout at their fellow passengers, who are given a wider berth? Or worse, what if she has already seen me and is now studying the ground-in gum and pigeon turds on her own platform, so that I don't call out in greeting?

As I'm getting up the courage, the trains start pulling in. This is always the case. Everyone shuffles aboard and takes their seats. As luck would have it, I end up directly across from this woman I used to know. I can see her through the dirty panes of the train windows. Still, I am afraid to stare at her for long, for fear I will catch her eye and have to do something silly on my side of the glass — to indicate that

I know her, that all is forgiven, if forgiveness is what she wants, that no one could possibly remember that night back in college when she drank a pint of Jack Daniels on a dare and kissed everyone who came into range — myself included. But of course, I remember. And this will make any such gesture even harder to pull off — without words, without sound, through the dingy panes of the train windows so full of travelers' breath and hair grease.

The bells of the closing doors go off. Then our trains begin moving in opposite directions, or maybe it's only hers, and I see her face peer into a book or perhaps her lap, in an effort to keep the past where it has lain — since that moment before I woke when she stumbled from my bed and stopped attending the Shakespeare class, the one where she sat beside me, and would ask to copy my notes.

***

Rain

This morning it rained in broad daylight. A father was headed to the bus stop, a daughter on either side of him, down the maple-lined suburban road it was getting hard to live on. They walked down the center of it because they could. The only neighbor who drove too fast was already gone, his red pickup missing from the tire-worn patch of lawn where he parks it.

"It's raining," said the daughter to his left. The soft rope of her ponytail swung back and forth as her gaze flicked from one side of the street to the other.

And it was. Though the sky was a clear September blue, the trees were shedding a little storm. They heard it on both sides of the street — the pattering of drops as they leapt from leaf to leaf to lawn. But they could see it only to the left of them — where the sun had play and could ignite the falling drops like dust motes clapped from a window-side couch.

"It's just the dew," he said, regretting, as he said it, the way he'd reduced it to a fact.

"Why is it falling?" said the daughter to his right. She adjusted the strap of her backpack and looked into his eyes, expecting nothing more than the perfect answer — one that made sense, one she could understand.

For this he was less quick. The air was breezeless — even the air high above them seemed still. A single contrail failed to lose any of its distinctness as they moved up the middle of that tiny storm. It made him think of a hurricane's eye — that clarity when people come out to sightsee and get killed, because they forget the rest is coming.

"I don't know," he said. "Maybe it is the rain. Maybe the drops have been hiding in the leaves from the last time. Maybe the sunlight chased them out." He was happy to hear at least a hint of something in his own voice that showed the world didn't always turn out to be the way it looked. He followed the contrail until it disappeared in the glare of the sun caught in the vines of bittersweet that rise like a tangled cloud in the crown of their neighbor's cherry tree.

His daughters weren't listening though. They were opening the umbrellas they carried in their backpacks. They were marching under the sugar maples just starting to bloody themselves with autumn. They were laughing and twirling the umbrellas at their friends, who stood at the treeless bus stop in bright light and shirtsleeves — not getting the joke, not understanding rain can fall from even cerulean skies.

Right now, his daughters' mother was headed south, possibly forever. When they asked about her missing car, their father told them it was in the shop. Later, he told them that their mother had gone on a trip, that the plane was the kind that left in the night to save on gasoline, that she would call when she landed. Lying to them was easy. Their ability to believe him unconditionally was one thing he hadn't squandered.

Two blue jays dove through the trees screaming, zigzagging so abruptly he thought they'd have to be connected to follow so well. They did it without hitting a branch, not even a leaf. Higher up, a buzzard wheeled over the street and flapped its sails twice, searching for an updraft so it could find the pets and half-domesticated possums that had been impulsive in the night.

His daughters were running now. At the same time, they were struggling to close up their umbrellas and stow them for when they would really need them — somewhere among the books and lunchbox, the extra house key, the list of emergency numbers, the family picture where they're all waving from the lip of a hotel balcony. They could hear the bus's bad engine climbing the hill. And then the yellow lights, the squeal of brakes, the mechanical stop sign that pops out like a toy.

The cars backed up in both directions — everyone smoking or angry or bored. And then the father waved to his daughters as he always did, and as often happened, they weren't looking — because their friends were happy and hearing the joke about the spinning umbrellas, the sunny rain.

He turned. He walked home in what was falling for reasons he couldn't understand. He sat down at the kitchen table with the phone in front of him. He was waiting for the call he knew would come — the call that would answer nothing, but that would have to be heard, ridden out, repeated.

***

Dance Lesson

His daughter is doing pliés to a slow brook of piano music behind the studio door. It is Saturday morning, and he is hungover, just like the other parents waiting in baseball caps and sweats.

Although the studio has a window, no one can see into it. There is a larger window that faces the parking lot, where the risen sun is blazing, turning the studio window into a mural of shifting cars. The lot and the window are milling with arrivals.

The woman in the corner pretending to read the paper looks like she may have been crying before she got here. A man on the opposite bench has a gut so big his t-shirt barely covers it, and he's scratching at a stained spot above his left knee. The rest of the parents stare into their phones.

Together, they feel the floor move as each child runs and leaps and lands in a wash of tinkling piano notes. In the mural, a woman rolls down her window and blows out a giant puff of smoke, as if the interior of the car were on fire. Her cigarette is amplified by the frozen breath of January.

During this quiet, headachy time, he likes to go over the past week's failures, the future week's triumphs. What else should he be thinking about? Don't mountain climbers pause to collect their wits on the last ledge before the summit? Don't we all have a box where the bills can gather before we try to pay them?

Behind the studio door, the daughters of his town are learning to be graceful, practicing the moves they will eventually string together for a two-minute recital in June. He believes his daughter is looking for him looking at her. He can feel it. So for her sake, he smiles into the mural of parking cars at the point where a man is taking his daughter's hand and running for the door.

***

LATE

He couldn't sleep. He was sure his wife was cheating on him, that if she came home at all, it would be to pack up all her things. He poured another drink and sat on the piano stool, stared into the darkened picture window behind the couch, and waited for her car. He saw himself inside of it. Hunched over, defeated. Ready to be struck by a shovel. Just then, across the street and inside of where his face was floating, the floodlights tripped on above his neighbor's garage. A possum waddled across his neighbor's driveway to the green plate of her acorn-filled yard. But then the possum stopped, looked over its shoulder, and ran like hell toward the woods on the opposite side of the house, the floodlights igniting one by one until the yard was blazing as it entered the blackness of the woods. Whatever spooked it never showed itself. He watched until each of her lights clicked off again in reverse order. Nothing but stars and doorbells, from one end of the street to the other.

Her Dinner

The woman I used to love is in another city, making her dinner of steak and boiled potato. It is almost certain that she is not thinking of me, who was just one of many lovers she'd had near the beginning of her long life of affairs and one-night stands. Probably she is married now, and her husband is away on business, which is why she turns in the pan a single portion of flank steak, and pokes with a fork her one potato to see if it is done.

It is not easy to imagine that she is alone on a permanent basis — this woman whose erotic life I was unable to keep pace with, who is still shapely enough to turn the heads in the aisles of her supermarket. Surely, her husband is on his way. Perhaps he is up in the air right now, flying towards her from another continent, and she is making this dinner so she will be sustained, so that when he barges into their apartment in the morning she will have the strength to ravish and be ravished.

Now, she is draining the water from around her potato, holding it back with a fork, for it is too fragile to be speared and taken out. It must be rolled out of the pot with a watery thud. She is arranging the meat upon her plate and, touchingly, breaking off a sprig of the parsley she has growing on the windowsill beside the drain board.

When she cuts into the meat and the blood seeps out, I am satisfied — because nothing could ever stay hidden from her. The world once leapt to her tongue to be tasted, and there is a part of me, perhaps many parts, that hopes it will always be thus.

***

Tornado

We awoke at 2:37 a.m. to the sound of trains in a town where there were no trains. I was a little drunk and I wanted to ignore it, to burrow back down to sleep. A minute later, though, the wind was louder than any I'd ever heard.

"Get up," Sara said.

Our bedroom windows opened out. It was pouring now, and hailing. And there was enough lightning that I decided it wasn't worth it to close them. That's how loud and flickering it was. I wouldn't stick my hand six inches outside to pull a window shut. It felt unwise, like trying to pull an apple peel out of a running garbage disposal.

This all happened in Arkansas. Sara and I were living on the second floor of a rickety three-story apartment building. The walls were little better than draperies. In the six months we'd been there, we'd heard every turd, whimper, sexual grunt, and curse that our neighbors had to offer. The only thing resembling a basement was the laundry room, but we'd have to run outside and down the stairs to get to it.

"Let's get in the closet," Sara said. Someone had told us you should wedge yourself into the smallest possible space. Bathrooms were supposed to be good because, it was said, the pipes and tub would create a kind of roll cage when the house exploded. Our bathroom touched an outside wall, though, and we thought better of it. So into the closet we went. And in a fit of genius, I pulled the mattress off our bed and dragged it inside as far as it would go. I wedged myself sideways into Sara's lap with the towels slipping off the top shelf onto our heads. We could barely move.

"The birds! We forgot the birds!" Sara said. She was talking about the two parakeets I'd bought the week she moved down here from New Jersey. They were a kind of consolation prize for leaving her friends and family and job and hair stylist a thousand miles away. To be with me. The man who drank too much, the man who had been cheating on her almost since he had met her.

"There's no time," I said.

"I'll get them," she shouted. "Let me out." She began squirming beneath me, searching for a way to get out from underneath the grand piano I'd become.

"I can't get up," I lied. "The mattress is stuck."

Then the power went out, and for the next thirty or forty

seconds, I pretended to try to move the mattress while she said things like "Hurry!" and "We're running out of time!" and "It's okay, birdies. It'll be okay." The parakeets were thrashing and banging inside their blanket as if they were under attack.

And then the wind cut off and it became normal rain, and I continued to pretend to be stuck for another half a minute.

We found some birthday candles in the kitchen, and I stuck one in each of the half-eaten dinner rolls I pulled out of the trash. I handed one to Sara, and she spent the next ten minutes cooing at the birds to calm them. Their feathers were all over the floor. They clung to the side of the cage and had wild accusatory eyes.

I couldn't find my cigarettes, so I fished a half-smoked butt out of the ashtray and began to straighten it. Sara came into the kitchen to get another candle.

"You left the birds out on purpose," she said. "You could have gotten up. You're a pussy."

Somebody snickered in the apartment to our left. I couldn't deny it. I grabbed a beer and pushed myself into the couch. As I lay there, the couples to the left and right made love. There was even a squeaking bed frame from the apartment above us where an old man lived by himself.

Sirens were in the distance. I considered the blackness of our apartment. Sara and I were having one squabble after another. It was tiresome. My thoughts drifted toward Rachel and what it must be like in her own apartment across town. Was she alone? Was she wearing what I liked? Was she thinking of me thinking of her in the wreckage of our town?

In the morning, we saw the giant oak toppled across our parking lot's only exit. It was full of wires. We heard that the preacher's house two blocks over was the only one destroyed. We rationed water. We used the toilet at the Texaco station.

It took until the next morning for the chainsaw crews to make it to our parking lot, and by then she was packed, birds and all. Hers was the first car out.

***

II.

ORCHARD BRIGHT

Some people swore that the house was haunted. Some people said it was just the wind. It rose out of the hill like a hunk of pale sky — the original blue still visible where a shutter had fallen off. A rabble of apple trees surrounded the house.

I lived in the Orchard Bright development, just below it. There was an apple tree in every yard. I suppose the developers wanted people to believe they had spared a tree for each of us from the original farm. The houses were clean and new. My own still smelled faintly of fresh paint. But the development had street names like Mountainview Road and Paradise Lake Lane. There were no mountains, and the lake was bottomed by concrete.

Scarlett lived up in the haunted house. I liked her because she smiled at me even when I didn't deserve it. She let me kiss her as her mother patrolled the lower floors with a dust rag and vacuum. We sat upstairs on her bedroom rug, listening to the radio, adjusting the little knobs.

Scarlett told me that once, late at night, footsteps had marched back and forth in the attic above her bed. She said it was the ghost of something beautiful. That's where some people said the guy hung himself. Some people said the guy was Scarlett's father.

One night I snuck into Scarlett's room. A half-moon was caught in the telephone wires. I told Scarlett I loved her. She told it back to me, but she said it with tears. Like love was a burden, like I was something she couldn't get her arms around — a washing machine, a grand piano.

Some people said Scarlett slept around, that all you had to do was knock. Maybe that was true but I didn't care. I figured she was searching for the guy who could rescue her, who could steal her away from that azure house, the house where her crazy father had died and where her mother kept prowling in search of dust.

Scarlett asked me how could I love her. I didn't understand. That was like asking how apples knew it was time to leave the tree. They just did — when they were ripe, when the sky was closing in. But Scarlett wasn't prone to accepting the irrefutable. She told me we were wrong for each other. She told me to stay the night.

I was crying now too. Nothing made sense. She was asking me to stay and telling me to leave. And yes, by "stay," I mean to make love. And by "make love," I mean for the first time. And by "the first time," I mean to turn each other to shivers in a rickety house while her mother stayed up smoking with Johnny Carson, and the thud of raccoons or her father's feet kept stumbling above us, as he tested the beams for strength.

Then we fell off the bed and broke a table. And the TV cut off below us and the pacing stopped, and her mother came screaming up the stairs. I climbed half-naked through her bedroom window, deeply in love, and ran down to my house in Orchard Bright, where the apple trees once were full of bees.

I stood on the back lawn, watching Scarlett's house for some kind of sign, thinking she would wave from her window at the dark. She didn't. And eventually the lights of that old blue house went out, one by one by one. Nothing was ever the same again after that.

***

Saturday Night at Magellan's

"I saw your Sally in Frank's office. Better keep an eye on that one," said Fat Michael, dragging his fork through a plate of pasta.

Fat Michael was headwaiter at Magellan's, and he'd ridden me all summer. I was the college boy. The know-nothing. The dope who would depart in August, leaving Fat Michael to wait tables until he died.

"Sally's not doing anything with Frank," I said.

He forked a coil of angel hair into his mouth. "If it were me, I would check to make sure the gift stays wrapped." He said this with a smirk, which he buried in another forkful of pasta.

Sally was the hostess at Magellan's. Everyone knew I was in love with her, including Sally. But she was 23 and I was 19, and those four years meant a lot. Sally had a car, an apartment, a life; I had acne and a room in my parents' house. Now Fat Michael's words were like a cigarette stubbing out in my heart.

I banged out the swinging doors that led from the kitchen to the hallway and Frank's office. The laughter of the cooks waxed and waned as the doors swayed into place behind me. When I got there, the door was closed. I turned back to see Fat Michael's face blooming inside one of the kitchen door portholes. Then I knocked, more lightly than I meant.

"Not now," came the flat reply. There was something about the silence after he said this, like more than one person trying to keep quiet. I thought of the scent of Sally's shampoo, the clean strawberry wake of it. I knocked again. This time louder.

"There's a problem, Frank," I lied. I looked over my shoulder. Fat Michael's face floated there, chewing.

I heard Frank cursing under his breath as the chair pushed out. He cracked the door enough for me to see his face. "What is it? What's the big emergency?"

"Can I come in?" I asked.

Frank was a known cokehead. His nose was red, his collar flipped up. "No. I'm fucking busy. What's the problem?"

"It's the special," I said. "I don't think we have enough clams for the half-shells."

He rolled his eyes, "Just tell Alberto. He'll know what to do." He tilted up his watch. "I've got to make a call before we open." He was about to close the door, but checked himself, adding, "This isn't anything I need to know about." Then the door shut, and I heard the click of the latch fitting into the jamb.

I stood there for a moment, but all I could catch was Frank's chair scraping back into place. Then a radio flipped on and some stations twirled by until he settled on one with distorted guitars.

When I looked again, Fat Michael was gone from the porthole, which didn't sit right with me — like he'd proven his point.

Down the hall was the replica of a ship's prow. It had one of those women that stop at the waist, her hair arranged in such a way as to cover her naked breasts. Magellan's had a maritime theme, and this prow used to be in the lobby. But too many kids took too much interest. Now it was something to worry beside, this woman faced into the wind — heedless of storms and reefs — while the coast of Spain sank into the sea behind her.

I worked at the knot in my apron string. I was still trying to get my nail into it when Frank emerged, fitting his necktie into place and prowling toward the kitchen. I kept my eyes on his door. I tried to not even blink. And just when I thought Fat Michael was full of shit, the doorknob turned and out came Sally, buttoning the last button of her blouse and walking rapidly toward the ladies' room at the other end of the hall.

I stepped out from behind the prow. "Sally," I said, too weakly to reach her. Then "Sally!"

But she had already pushed inside the ladies' room, and I stood in that hallway dumbfounded — like a man arriving at a dock too late, the ship he wanted already at sea, the last of its sails let out.

From the kitchen, Fat Michael was calling for an order of half-shells. For Magellan's was open, and our Saturday night had just begun.

***

She Had Been Drunk Exactly Twice

When the Marshalls parking lot was empty and Jeremy looked at it in profile, the whole world seemed slanted in such a way that things might start falling off. He sat in his car waiting for Miranda to pull in for her shift.

Jeremy heard her before he saw her. The music from Miranda's open car window rose and fell as she turned around the lot. He watched as she cut the engine and gathered up her things. She was the first employee to arrive, and Jeremy couldn't understand how her car could end up parked crooked.

Miranda began walking before she even closed her door. She seemed always to be moving in a direction before she had fully decided on it. Jeremy liked that she fixed her hair as she went, that the birds somewhere were singing — the parking lot sparrows that bathe in puddles tinged with motor oil and anti-freeze. He got out and stood by his own door, leaving it ajar.

"Miranda!" he called from across the lot. Jeremy was

parked over by Stop & Shop so that she wouldn't see him waiting. Now he worried that his voice wouldn't carry. He shouted again and the pendulum swing of her purse clicked off. She turned to face him across the blacktop just beginning to ripple with the May brightness of a Saturday morning.

Jeremy started into a shuffling jog. He felt it would be overly dramatic to leave her standing there for the time it would take to walk to her. And yet running full-bore didn't seem right either. So he shuffle-jogged over, unable to decide on the kind of face the moment demanded.

"I was waiting for you," he said breathlessly. "I thought we could talk."

"I've got to work," said Miranda, and began moving in that direction.

As he followed, he said, "It's just that I know. I know how you must feel." He fidgeted with the oversized glass emerald of his class ring, twisting it over and back across his knuckle.

Miranda stopped again. "I don't see how that's possible. And it's none of your business anyway." She said this looking directly into his eyes, as if she were training a dog she hadn't asked for, as if she meant to convey that the bed was off-limits. "I shouldn't have told you."

But Jeremy had something to say, and he'd been rehearsing it in the car since dawn. He didn't care that they were in high school or that the baby wasn't his or that they'd never even kissed. He was in love with Miranda — with her dimples, with the rope of her ponytail.

They had been at the same party three nights before, and Miranda was drunk enough to confide in Jeremy — the sensitive boy from her English class, and the only guy at the party who hadn't pawed at her. When Miranda told him she was pregnant and planning to get rid of it, he felt the blocks of his life falling into place. This was a girl he could rescue.

Other Marshalls employees were arriving now, pulling in through the parking lot's many entrances as if it were an ambush. Jeremy heard the jingle of the giant key ring as the manager opened the font door and blocked it ajar so that the cashiers could clock in and get ready for the day's raft of bargain shoppers.

"Just hear me out," said Jeremy, reaching for her arm, which she twisted from his fingers. Something in Jeremy told him to act right now, that if he didn't things would start rolling away and he'd never catch up.

"I want you to have the baby," he blurted. "I want to marry you." This did not resemble the speech he'd been rehearsing.

"Keep it down," she hissed and took an angry step in his direction. But then she laughed, derisively. Miranda was 17 and had lost her virginity just seven weeks earlier. She had been drunk exactly twice and had never read a book that wasn't assigned, but the baby in her belly had made her too wise, probably forever.

The manager was waiting. He jiggled the keys and kicked out the triangular block of wood. He gave Miranda a look that said she was late even if she wasn't, and that he couldn't stand there all morning.

"It's already taken care of," she whispered to Jeremy and then hurried inside.

Jeremy stood in the middle of all those slowly filling spaces. For a full minute, he watched the door that had shut between them. She was in there somewhere behind the giant south-facing windows tinted almost to the point of blackness so that the cashiers wouldn't roast in their polyester vests as they rung up the customers who switched price tags and hid underwear in the pockets of what they would pay for. He turned suddenly toward his car, the dinging of the door chime just audible, and scattered two sparrows that had been fighting over a french fry.

When Jeremy would look back on this day, years later, he remembered his possible life with Miranda sliding off the edge of the lot as if they lived on a table someone had begun to lift from a corner he couldn't see.

The following Monday morning, Miranda took another seat in English class, and her answers about Gatsby and Godot were as blunt and misguided as Jeremy's or anyone else's as they waited for the bell, any bell, to tell them the lesson was over.

***

SHE'LL BE HOME BEFORE JOHNNY CARSON COMES ON

Thomas sat in the loft of his father's barn and gazed at the patchwork fields and how the creek cut through them any old way it liked. The moon would be full that night, the silos empty. The road that ran along their property was carless, though a distant hum of interstate sometimes drifted by.

His sister Sheila had just had another breakdown. Their father had left that morning for Bound Brook, to clear out her apartment and pay her bills. She had lasted six months. Now she was being brought back. If Thomas stayed up in the loft all night, he'd eventually see the headlights of their father's truck — the pickup bed full of dirty clothes and knick-knacks, the medicine taking its toll.

Sheila and Thomas used to climb to the loft when they were younger. Underneath was a wagonload of rye. Over and over, Thomas saw her plunge into space with the kind of confidence that resides only in convicts and beauty queens. He would not jump himself.

"Don't be a pussy all your life," Sheila said the last time she had leaped. But she caught her arm on the wagon edge and snapped it. His father didn't believe Thomas when he claimed he hadn't jumped. It was too incredible — the older brother looking on while his sister tested the world. "Where would she get an idea like that?" their father wanted to know as he yanked the belt out of its loops and blocked the door.

There were no overhead lights in the barn. At night, if he wanted the cigarettes he'd hidden there, he would have to bring a flashlight. This made it ideal for Sheila. She could see their father coming from across the yard with his lantern and his gun.

Thomas had found his sister there one night. The quiet of the barn told him right off that someone was inside. The beam raked over the tractor, the bales, the worktable full of things in need of adjustment, things that could cut or dig. And there was Sheila astride Bobby Minch, older even than Thomas. They shouted at him to get the hell out, and there was laughter when he did. Later that night, Sheila banged open his bedroom door and threw the cigarettes into his face.

Thomas began locking his door after that. Sheila would pound on it whole minutes at a time, but he had learned that silence — like the sound of a barn around two lovers — eventually sent her away.

And away she went. First to Summit, then to Little Falls, and then to Bound Brook. But she always came back.

The creek was fat. If they got more rain, it would slip right over the bank and make the southern field unplantable. Thomas counted four jets up in the sky — high and silent and silver, all headed off in their own direction.

He descended the ladder, and was careful when he came to the rung that had needed a new nail for years. At the house, the screen door whined open to reveal his mother, dusted with flour, working at a counter full of "welcome home" pies.

"Isn't it wonderful your sister's coming home?" she said. He didn't ask, but she told him anyway. "She'll be home before Johnny Carson comes on. We can all watch together."

"I'm not sure when I'll be back," he said.

Thomas took his car key off the hook. He wondered if his sister would know him as he traveled toward her at full speed, and then away from her just as fast.

***

From Hammonton, New Jersey: The Land of Berries

The summer we lost a dozen chickens to a fox, Momma made Daddy build her a brand-new henhouse. It was the same summer Amanda learned she was to leave for Ohio. She had never been out of South Jersey, but Amanda had cousins she'd be living with. She said Ohio was full of factories. Amanda was a year older than me, and smart. She knew all about my teachers before I had them, and she could make the change in her head at McCallister's corner store even faster than the register. But Ohio made Amanda quiet.

Once, Amanda and me were in the tractor barn in early spring, patching up holes in some irrigation pipe. There were birds building nests all over the rafters — quick scissory birds that never let you see their eyes. I touched my hand on the back of Amanda's neck and she flinched, like my fingers were hot. Momma told me I'd scare girls if I touched them with my burn hand. A long time ago, I took hold of the red coil of the kitchen stove. I don't remember this myself, but the coil is still in my palm. Momma says they had to pry my hand from it, and the doctor told her later some pains are so big they can't be felt, that this was a mercy of God. Daddy says I'd seen something pretty and wouldn't let go. He says when I get big the girls had better watch out.

If I needed to fuss with something on the other end of the farm, Amanda would get me in the pickup and drive us out. I'd sit in the bed and watch the rows of blueberries make a pattern. The opening of the row would hit me, and suddenly I could see clear across the field. And just as quick it was gone, replaced by another — and another and another. Amanda said that's perspective — that things look different depending on where you are. When she caught me staring at her hair gathering the wind inside the pickup cab, I'd turn back to the berries, and feel the bumpiness of the flat place we drove across.

One Saturday we were unloading the bee boxes. Daddy rented them for the flower time. Amanda and me put one at the edge of every field. We did it at night so we didn't get stung. The bees were inside sleeping. We could have set them on fire and they still wouldn't come out. Amanda said that's why we didn't need nets or funny hats. We put them where we wanted, and when the sun heated up, the bees came out and said thank you to the fields. Blueberry flowers can tell the future. You can see the shape of the berry in the way their petals shut. In a little while, everything on Daddy's farm would be closing and tightening, getting sweet. When Daddy's berries are ready, they go all over the world — even Ohio. On the carton, it says "From Hammonton, New Jersey: The Land of Berries."

When the first full week of picking was done, Amanda took some whiskey to the bonfire. The fire was built from Momma's old henhouse. The new one stood like a palace outside my bedroom window. Fox-proof, she called it. I don't know why. It had a door. If I were a fox, I'd walk right in and slip a hen between my jaws, and then I'd slide like a knife into the berry rows in case Daddy came looking with his floodlight and his gun. Every now and then, a feather dislodged from one of the boards and shot up into the night. Sometimes on fire, sometimes not. Amanda handed me the bottle.

Amanda had a glassy smile. She took my good hand and led me into the rows of tomorrow's field. The berries brushed against us as we went. I grabbed a handful and got rid of the whiskey taste. Amanda called that a satisfaction. From the middle of the field, we could hear the crackle of the fire, and the people around the fire, talking and joking in Spanish. When somebody threw on a board, a fountain of sparks leapt up.

Amanda told me she was leaving for Ohio in the morning, that she'd never see me again. Then she told me her Momma had cancer somewhere in her belly, and that was the reason for Ohio. I wanted to cry at this, but Daddy says boys that cry are pussies. So I stood there listening to Amanda talk about the factories of Ohio, how they're so loud you can't hear the songs inside your own head, how sometimes men fall into the machines and get pressed into car parts or sausages, how it's too much trouble to fish them out. She said her cousins all worked in the factories. She said she'd be doing that too.

I reached out and touched Amanda's neck. The whiskey had made me forget, and I used my burn hand. She didn't flinch. And it was like the way I imagined that stove coil must have been all those years ago.

Somebody yelled in Spanish — angry or joking, I couldn't tell — and threw another chunk of henhouse onto the fire. I was so close to Amanda, I could see the sparks flying up in her eyes. The land of berries stretched into the night, and Momma's henhouse was almost gone. Somebody, I knew, would have to pry me from this girl.

***

I've Seen It in the Movies

Mark had bought a second-hand Comet with the money he'd saved working at McGettigan's Gas, so he and Margot would get in the car and drive through the sod farms and goldenrod of South Jersey, smoking cigarettes and laughing at the broken-down barns they lived among. The gas, after all, was free — Mark would sneak it off the pumps.

Eventually the fields gave way to pines, and they'd get on one of the sandy roads that led like a contrail into Wharton Forest. They'd drive in, park, and fool around until Margot decided he should stop. Sometimes they'd go skinny-dipping in the tea-colored rivers, and Mark would admire Margot and wonder why he was allowed to enjoy her body only from a distance.

One day, Margot didn't want to ride down the sandy roads into the pines. She kept talking about Auburn — the college she'd be leaving for in a couple of weeks. Mark liked the sound of the name because it was also the color of Margot's hair, but he hated everything else about it. Margot explained again how far away it was, how she wasn't sure she'd be able to fly back, even at Christmas.

They drove in silence for a while. Mark liked to pick a road he'd never been down and just keep going. He was a dog testing the limits of its leash. Towns sprang up and fell away. He wasn't sure where they were. Slowly, a new smell came in through the window — low-tide mud, brine.

"You've never been to the ocean?" asked Margot. She was incredulous and made him drive faster. "The ocean will blow your mind." She lit a cigarette for each of them and passed one over.

"I've seen it in the movies," he said.

They came to a bridge that lifted them into the overcast air above a bay. The marsh spread out beneath them.

"I'd like to walk out into that grass," Mark said.

"Don't," Margot scoffed. "You'd sink in up to your neck and drown when the tide came back." She blew a cloud of smoke out the window.

"It looks so pretty," he said.

"Only from far away," she said. "It's full of green flies and crabs." Then she added thoughtfully, "The people around here hate tourists. You have to not seem like a tourist."

After they parked, they walked over a small dune ribboned by hurricane fence with trash stuck all over it. The water was far away, and the wind made it hard to hear each other. It took their words and hurled them backward toward the car.

When they got to the tide line, Mark dipped his fingers in and tasted them. He had heard the water was salty, and was pleased at this confirmation. He wanted to drink a palmful of it, but Margot wouldn't let him.

"People pee in that water," she said.

The day was gray and threatening rain, and the beach was practically empty. The sun, if they could see it, would be setting soon. For twenty minutes the two of them walked along the water's edge, watching the ships move slowly across the bottom of the sky. Mark had heard that every ship flew a flag, but these were too far away to tell. Mark picked up an orange shell, the size and shape of a concave half-dollar.

"Do you know the name of this one?" he asked.

She didn't, and waved him off as she tried to light a cigarette in the relentless wind.

"Someday I'll go to Europe," said Margot when she finally got it going, looking out across the water where the ships were disappearing. "I'll stay in the top floors of the tallest hotels and drink mimosas all day long."

Mark had never thought about Europe. The farthest his mind had wandered was Auburn. He registered how unlikely it would be for him to ever get there, and it bothered him that he'd never known about the beach, the ocean, the vastness of the world he'd been living beside. His home was only two hours away. And that's when he knew he would never see Margot again. She was leaving him, and he would travel through the dark in his beat-up Comet, full to the brim with stolen gas, waiting for the road that would take him out of here.

***

The Blanket

Doreen had a bad reputation. The other girls gave you a look if they found out you'd spoken to her. But Doreen and I hung out together anyway at the Rosewood Country Club pool. She'd let me rub lotion into her back or change the station on her radio, and she didn't seem to mind that I enjoyed her from behind my sunglasses whenever she bent to pick up her towel.

Toward the end of summer, we agreed to sneak out one Saturday night and meet on the edge of the eighth-hole green. Before our date, I stashed a blanket in the woods, along with a bottle of Early Times, which I'd lifted from the crowd of my father's liquor cabinet.

That night, I slipped out and followed the creek to the spot where Doreen would be waiting like an X on an old-time treasure map. The trees along the way were towering oaks, the tallest in our town. They were full of fireflies, thousands of them, maybe a million. Sometimes they looked like a city seen from a plane, sometimes like the switchboard of god gone mad with prayer.

There was a dog barking somewhere near the horizon of sound when I arrived. Then Doreen stepped out of the woods with the half-finished bottle of Early Times. It took me a moment to realize she wasn't wearing any jeans. No skirt, no underwear. Nothing. She pulled me down to the blanket laid out beneath the shifting constellations of the fireflies.

Doreen and I spent the next hour fucking and drinking whiskey and crying and passing out and looking for our clothes. I walked her home and helped her through the bedroom window. By some miracle, the other windows of her house all stayed dark, even after she stumbled into what must have been her bed. Then I headed back along the dead August air of the creek.

The trees were dark. It was as if someone had kicked out the plug of the fireflies. I smelled my fingers. I licked my lips. Doreen was everywhere, and the stars had a watery look, like they were reflected in a puddle that an 18-wheeler was roaring past.

Doreen never spoke to me again, and I wondered for a day why I was so itchy. I didn't bother to retrieve the blanket from the woods, and I floated through the remaining days of summer with the weight of my virginity cast away at last. I went to college, took a job far away, got married, and took another job still farther. Then I came back for my 25th class reunion held at the Rosewood Country Club. That's when I learned that Doreen had killed herself after the rest of us went off to live our lives.

So now I'm out by the eighth-hole green, and the music of my lost virginity is drifting over the fairway to where I stand. I kick up the leaves until I find the blanket. It is still here, though 25 years of rain and rot have tried to turn it into dirt. I want to take it away with me, but a tree is growing through the middle of it. A thousand roots hook it into place. In the almost useless glow of my struck match, I see the confused milling of centipedes, the sluggish retreat of glistening worms.

***

The Grownups Came Out to See the Sky

Once, during the summer when I was thirteen, the grownups came out to see the sky. It was not a sunset that could properly be viewed from behind glass. Our stickball game stopped without any protest, and Billy Mutschler yelled for his sister to come out when he sensed that she might miss it. The neighborhood women drifted over the lawns, aproned and chatty, and from their doorsteps, the men tipped beers at each other in a tired salute. We kids kept ogling and pointing, waiting for the sunset to pass over our game as if it were a thundershower. Then Billy's sister came out on her porch and stood beside her father. She was swept up in the sky and couldn't see that I was watching her. I noted the pinkness of her exposed bra strap, that it was the same shade battering out of the clouds just then. For what must have been five minutes, the sky blazed above the mortgages we didn't understand, and under which the fathers were laboring, even then.

***

The Ring

Maureen is 16. She was told to leave it alone — the band of bloody garnets and real gold her older sister kept in the jewelry box in the back of her keepsake drawer. A boy had given it to her — her first real ring — but then he moved away.

For two days Maureen has hidden the ring beneath a band-aid. It is flesh-colored. It allows her to sit with her sister at dinner, unsuspected.

Maureen tries everything she can think of to get it off: soap, olive oil, Vaseline — even canola oil because she thought the lightness of it might mean it's more slippery. She tries icing her hand and heating it up, hours of twisting and pulling. She has to stop when she feels her knuckle dislocating. The skin is chafed and raw around the ring. It swells to hold the gold even more tightly.

"Maybe your sister won't notice it's missing," I offer.

Maureen shrugs. "She'll see it's gone. She'll know it was me. She caught me trying it on before."

"Why doesn't she wear it?"

"It doesn't fit."

This makes us laugh, and I draw her to me. I kiss her and paw at the outside of her sweater until she pushes me away.

Maureen tells me the boy is coming back from far away to visit. Her sister will want the ring.

"But it doesn't fit," I say.

"She'll wear it on a chain around her neck. She did it the last time he came back."

So we go to the mall. There's a jewelry store there, and we think that maybe they have a cream, some trick we could buy to remove the ring. The car is Maureen's, but she always makes me drive. She says a man should never be seen getting driven around by a woman. It's an old Buick that rattles as we idle at the lights. It stalls if I give it the gas too hard.

"You'll have to cut it off. It's the only way," says the jeweler. He is kindly and old and seems to have encountered this very predicament many times before.

Maureen winces as he forces the snip between her skin and the gold. When it finally clicks through, a garnet bounces over the display glass. The jeweler pries it apart and she's free. She wiggles her finger and smiles.

The old man has a ring in the case that's a close match. It has one garnet less, and it's a size smaller. Maureen says it's close enough, and I hand over the $64.99 I'd been saving from my paper route. I have it inscribed "To my beloved."

I slip the ring onto Maureen's pinky. "Only halfway!" she warns, because now she's learned her lesson. It seems momentous though — the way slipping a ring on a girl always does. Like there's a marriage in the gesture.

When we get back to the car, I pull Maureen to me, thinking I've got some kind of thank-you coming my way — seeing how I bought her the ring and saved the day and fixed it so her sister would never know. She lets me kiss her, but when I start with her sweater, she pushes me away.

"Not here," she says. "Not now."

I look around. The mall parking lot in the deepening dusk has never looked better, but I've already been to the edge of this particular fence enough times to know that there are no gaps.

So we get in the Buick, and I start it to rattling. I take her home with the ring on her pinky so she can give it back to the hidden jewelry box, so that her sister can tell the boy she wears it every day — on a chain, because that's what the girls are doing this year, because that's how much she loves him.

***

Engagement

The Gulf War began as Jake and Christine were registering for their wedding at Macy's. They were busy with china patterns and appliances they would never use. Jake understood this in a way that Christine did not. Why would they want to make their own bread? Could someone really tell the difference between mixed and pureed? Jake peered into the shelves for a blender with just one button.

Suddenly all the TVs along the wall in the home entertainment room were full of tracer bullets and minarets. Baghdad was on fire. The pictures were a grainy, night-vision green. It reminded Jake of the fireflies he and his friends used to grind into the sidewalks of his boyhood. A seasonal graffiti.

Thankfully, Jake and Christine didn't know anyone who'd been deployed — they barely knew each other. They had met six months ago and been foolish in bed. Now Christine was pregnant. The engagement would be brief.

Christine tried to draw Jake back to the items they needed to choose. She said something mysterious about thread counts. But Jake stepped to the side of her without answering. He wanted to watch the war.

A woman nearby began crying. She said her son was over there, up in the sky where all the tracer bullets were headed. She said this to no one and to everyone. Jake edged away. She seemed old. It was hard to think of her holding a boy to her breast. Christine wished she could comfort this woman, but she didn't see how that was possible.

More and more shoppers lined up in front of the 37 televisions shifting and flickering in unison. Nobody paid attention to the rogue "Wheel of Fortune" in a corner of the room that one of the sales ladies must have been planning to watch. It was all set up like a giant living room, with couches and end tables. Nobody sat though. The room was full of something like excitement — the big game finally starting. They had expected it to start, of course. The president had drawn a line. He had set a date. He had moved an army to the other side of the world.

A baby in a stroller was aimed at Jake. His mother had had the sense to face him away from the news, though she herself kept watching. Jake assumed it was a boy. His face was uncommonly pretty, yet the mother had ensconced him in blue — hat, gloves, pants, coat. Even a blue blanket for him to hold. He looked like an angel pushed around in a carriage full of sky.

Christine put an arm around Jake's waist and smiled into the carriage. The baby was cute. The sounds he made reminded her of a puppy she'd had as a girl. She thought how agreeable it would be to have a baby in their apartment. Jake thought of puppies too — of fleas and piss, and vomit behind the couch. Then there was a large green flash — a missile arriving from hundreds of miles away from the deck of a ship attacking a desert.

The room filled up with sirens and shaky camera footage and the escalating panic in the correspondent's voice. After all, he was in a hotel at the center of a city that was burning down around him. Nothing was clear. No one could see the planes these bombs were falling from. They detonated without warning as if they had always been there, as if they were part of the city itself.

The baby in the carriage sighed and gurgled. He slobbered on his fist and kicked. He looked from the crying woman, to Christine, and finally to Jake. He craned his neck as if searching for his mother. No one paid attention. Then, he threw his rattle on the floor and heard it skitter like a mouse over the linoleum he could not see.

Everyone turned and followed the arc of the spinning rattle. The woman who had been crying for her son the pilot picked it up and gave it to the young mother. The mother thanked her, and the rattle descended back to the baby, as he must have known it would, from the sky above his carriage, by means of the disembodied hand he knew to be his mother's. Nobody thought this at the time, of course, but there was something unsettling about a sky that let down rattles as easily as bombs. Or rain. Or hailstones. Or toads.

Christine leaned into Jake, as if to emphasize the rightness of their choices. Jake kept scanning the screens, somehow surprised by what already had become predictable footage. The war had arrived and nobody moved. They had resolved, en masse and without discussion, to wait for the first commercial.

***

III.

Rio de Janeiro

He flew to Rio without her, believing this trip, like certain cliffs, would give him perspective. He saw the famous statue of god and the slums beneath it climbing. The tiniest birds were beggars, the sun cruel. Everywhere the women ignored his tourist Portuguese. Everywhere the poor were hungry, and had steady eyes. The eyes of god were steady too — but on the horizon, where now and then the bottom of a boat was eaten by the world.

***

My Yoga Pants, My Executioner

You laugh, but I was once the most sought after male yoga pants model in the world — not just Rhode Island, not just the Eastern seaboard. The world.

It was back in the 80s, when yoga pants were first catching fire. I was the go-to model for solids. True, I'm a little flabby now, but I was a god back then — like Michelangelo's David dipped into ink or azure sky or the yellow tongue of a candle's flame. They gave the leopard prints and camouflage to the models with stubby legs and ankles full of spider veins. To everyone else, is what I mean.

Jacques was my rival and my downfall. He was the French male yoga pants model, and everyone fell in love with his clove cigarettes, the pretentious way he had of going by just his first name — like he was Cher or Twiggy.

Let's face it. It was a woman's world. The yoga pants catalogues rarely needed more than one male model. Oh, we did some shoots together — Jacques and I. But the money was always looking for something vaguely homoerotic.

They were pushing the envelope, and it's one of the reasons that even today the yoga pants industry is seen as a pioneer in gay friendliness.

Anyway, I couldn't pull it off. I remember the exact moment things went bad, and I felt my career turning like a ship toward the reef that had always been there. Jacques was doing the downward dog at sunset on a beach in Bora Bora. We'd waited all afternoon for the light to be right, and then they passed me a bottle of Bain de Soleil and told me to rub it into his back. Jacques was hairy. Too hairy. All the French male models acted like they'd never heard of waxing. It was revolting to have my fingers on him. I ended up looking like someone who had walked in on a dissection, or like I'd been given a live cricket to eat. The light changed. The shoot was ruined. And I flew home to a phone that never rang again.

Jacques rode the craze for all he was worth, and I won't begrudge him that. I had lived at the very core of the yoga pants world, and understood its fierce allure — the private jets, the champagne breakfasts, the pedicures, the countless women reaching for a touch. But it was work too. On the yoga pants circuit, life was an endless schedule of squats and treadmills, tofu and grapefruit juice.

Then Richard Simmons got popular, and the bottom fell out. Everyone wanted baggy striped shorts, which in my opinion are just too forgiving. He was essentially promoting being out of shape. It was a lazy man's fitness.

Although I couldn't get work, I still had my money. But I was too young to handle it. My father was a banker and I could have used his advice, but we were on the outs back then. He had wanted a son who played football or who joined the Marines — not a son who rocked the camera in yoga pants. So I was left with the advice of the only people I trusted — my stylist and my whole-foods consultant. Unfortunately, they said to put the money into Swatches and leg warmers. And I did. But I bought high, and had to sell low. It's an old story.

I don't even wear yoga pants anymore. Too many memories. Too many ghosts. I went through a period of heavy drinking, but eventually I picked myself up, went back to college, and took my degree in marine science. In fact, I'm packing for a trip right now to study the turtles of Bora Bora. I'd be lying if I didn't admit to some misgivings. Returning to those beaches after all these years will be a lot like the soldiers going back to Normandy, I imagine. It's going to hurt, but I feel like I'm ready (fingers crossed).

As for Jacques, I heard he overdosed at a Boy George after-party. This was during the comeback tour. They found him facedown and shirtless beside his works, wearing a pair of motley stirrup pants. He still didn't believe in waxing, and stirrup pants — for god's sake — should only be worn as solids.

Jacques, oh Jacques! Even I never hoped you would fall so far.

***

The Secret Thoughts of Thomas, the Clerk in Men's Wear

Thomas had spent the afternoon folding shirts in the men's department. Christmas would be upon them soon, and the store was always busy. Sometimes, he would just finish folding a sweater when a woman grabbed it and shook it out, holding it up to the air as if it were her husband. Then she'd frown and drop it back to the table in a heap. At such times, Thomas remembered the stories of planes breaking apart high above the earth, how the rushing air would peel the clothing from the passengers, how they would end up naked and dead on the forest floor, how their clothes would hang in the branches for miles — like Christmas ornaments put up by a drunk. He imagined the clothes in the highest branches were simply left in place. Someone could die just trying to retrieve them, he reasoned. Years later, though, when the crash was forgotten and the loggers inevitably arrived, somebody's auburn pencil skirt would tell them what happened here, if only they could listen. The faded blazers

and underwear would suddenly be back on solid ground —
the accident over at last.

***

Europe Is the Invention of Americans

There is no Europe. I've been saying this for years, much to my wife's discomfort at cocktail parties and reunions.

"But I've been to France," she insists. "I inhaled the yeast-iness of bakery bread as I walked through an alley down which could be seen the apex of the Eiffel Tower."

I'm not buying it. As far as I'm concerned, the Atlantic Ocean just keeps going.

"Where do you think we came from?" she asks, trying to see if I'll repeat her propaganda about Luxembourg and Spain and the huddled masses.

"Adam and Eve," I tell her. I don't really think this of course, but it shuts her up. The people who believe in Europe tend to believe in the Bible. They have the same need for there to be something farther than the horizon. Clouds aren't good enough for them.

I say Europe is the invention of Americans whose mistakes are so bad, so big, so colossal, they want for them to have happened on the other side of the world. Haven't you ever noticed that Louisiana and Italy both look like a boot stepping into a puddle, that Kentucky and Austria are basically the same shape? Palaces and queens and the Magna Carta — the whole thing stinks of fairy tales.

When I talk like this, my wife exhales and begins swirling the ice in her drink. That's when I remind her of Las Vegas.

"That wasn't Europe," she snaps.

"Exactly," I say. "That's where you had to sell your body for airfare after you went crazy with the credit cards while I slept off a quart of Cutty Sark. Remember? Two men took you by storm in that hotel from which could be seen the apex of the Eiffel Tower."

She glares at me as if I've been talking about her flatulence. The people beside us start looking around like this might be the kind of party where waiters go weaving through the crowd with little trays of olives and crabmeat.

"I'm sure you remember," I say. "Later that night, we saw the New York City skyline winking in the desert air after I vomited into that fountain at the Bellagio. You said you were ashamed. You said you were sorry."

"We're not talking about that now," she hisses and begins shaking her purse for her cigarettes, peering into it as if there's a television at the bottom with bad reception.

This is her way of letting me know I've won, that she'll stop insisting openly about such fantasies. At least for a while she'll agree with me that Europe is a land of watered-down drinks and palm trees, call girls and slot machines that take your money in increments. Or, if you're at the right table, you can lose it all at once, though this takes foresight and effort — the kind that can conjure a continent from seawater and smog.

As for the different languages — another misapprehension. Those are just very thick American dialects. You can figure them out if you really try. As I always say, America is big. Even the President doesn't know where all the roads are leading, despite his having built them.

**

They Had Wandered Out of Frame

Charles was a writer, and Laura was an accountant. They made a video once, a sex video. He had set up a small camera in the fake plants on top of the armoire beside his bed. He was careful to put a piece of black tape over the red light that said the camera was recording.

The movie was not what Charles expected. When he watched it later that night, alone, after Laura had gone home, he saw that he was more selfish than he knew, that she was less ecstatic than he remembered. They huffed and gasped as if they were competing in a triathlon.

By the second half of the tape, they had wandered out of frame. Only his own ass was visible, pumping away at a woman the camera could not see. It could have been anyone, and if you had begun watching in the last moments of the film, you might even guess he was alone. The money shot could only be heard — like someone being stabbed. It hadn't helped that he'd been drinking.

Now, Charles and Laura were broken up, and had been

so for several months. They had both met and discarded other people, and were well past the point of getting back together. He wondered what he should do with the tape, which he hadn't looked at since that first night. To destroy it seemed impetuous. He remembered how badly he felt after he'd thrown away his childhood stamp collection. Years later, his niece took an interest, and he wished he had those old stamps back so he could share them.

To give Laura the tape was reckless. He was sure she'd be angry. Weeks after he'd made the recording, he suggested openly that they set a camera up one night (believing her cooperation would increase the production values). She was against it categorically. In fact, the broaching of the subject seemed to be a catalyst for their eventual separation. Besides, he came off badly in the film, and he had a secret wish for all of his ex-lovers to remember him fondly, someday.

But keeping it for himself, up in the closet, beside the stack of *Playboys* from the year he'd had a subscription, also felt unsatisfying. This was the kind of thing you were supposed to tell people about — it was like getting a hole in one, or seeing a bald eagle for the first time, or meeting Madonna on the subway.

So Charles did the only thing he knew. He wrote a story about the tape in the third person and published it in a small midwestern journal. If ever he were asked if the story were true, he decided he would be evasive. He would take pleasure in insisting that he was a writer of fiction, that the lived life had little to do with the imagined life. Because he enjoyed being difficult and casting doubt on all he said, he didn't bother to change Laura's name or his own. He hoped that she would find a copy of it, by chance, in the magazine rack of her local bookstore. Or maybe a friend from the Midwest would mail it to her with the first page folded down and a note that said, "Didn't you used to date this guy?" And for a few moments, Laura would put aside her spreadsheets and calculations to think about him, to remember the feel of his hands on her body, to recall the taste of his kiss.

When his contributor's copy arrived in the mail, he placed it on the coffee table as a conversation piece. That night, the tape went into the fire he'd built in the backyard pit. It was suddenly the only option. He watched the particles of their half-hearted contortions rise like a fat and unclimbable rope to the stars above his yard, the ones he had always said reminded him of Laura's eyes as they lay together in the dark after making what he thought was love — even when they didn't, even when her eyes were shut.

***

STAMINA

As they make love, he thinks of spreadsheets and Visa bills, the spinning wheels of the electricity meter stuck to the wall of their house. To do otherwise is to give in to his wife's beauty, and that would never do. For once he comes, he falls instantly to sleep, and his wife would be left dissatisfied in their palace of disordered sheets.

It had been a problem from their earliest days together. In college, once, he came just from the act of slipping on a condom. Had he not mastered himself, he felt sure she would have left him, that they would not have their son and daughter, the attic window from which they could see the ocean sparkling between evergreens, or the cat that curls into their bed each night.

Now they are switching positions, which is always tricky for him — a time when he must be vigilant. Things are going well. His wife is responsive. She is doing that thing where she props one leg over his shoulder and encourages him to lean into her. But he must think of dissections when she does this — how back in biology class he pulled two grasshoppers and a crayfish from the stomach of the bull-frog pinned to the tray of wax.

She is beginning to pant and make noises she later will be embarrassed by. He has to stopper his ears against such music. So he imagines the corpses at Dachau bulldozed into an open pit, the twin towers imploding, a fox leg getting left behind in the jaws of a steel spring trap. It is too much, but his wife has gotten everything she needs, and he lets go of himself for the briefest moment.

They lie together gasping in the jumbled bed and the gathering dusk. A dog down the street is barking. The man's sleep approaches like a loaded barge fitting against a dock. He pulls his wife close and thinks, as he sometimes does, that sex is different from what he imagined back in high school, as he flipped through the pages of *Penthouse* and *Swank*.

He turns over to look into his wife's eyes, but already she is asleep. He is alone with the crickets coming on like little switches in the moat of roses surrounding their house. He is about to slip off himself when the cat leaps softly onto their bed, curling in between them in its usual spot.

***

THIEF

He stole the stars above her house, pulling them out with a claw hammer. She wouldn't love him anymore, so he left her with a blue-black vault of night — the color of the grackles he used to throw rocks at as they crowded out the other birds around their backyard feeder.

He wanted her to see that the sky had been looted. She never noticed though, because already she had taken a lover, and why would she need the sky and its Rorschach of light when she had a man to pin her to the bed each night?

Meanwhile, the stars were back at his place. It was hard to sleep with the glow of them leaking out of his dresser drawers and the bed too big without her. So off he'd go to the couch, which at least reminded him of the times when she had lived there.

Some nights, he'd get up, walk across town, and climb into the crook of her backyard maple — the one with a view of her curtains and the shadow play of bodies.

One night he waited for the other man's car to leave.

Then he reached into his pocket for the pebbles. The first one hit the window and the light came on. She peered into the night, and didn't seem to notice it was a tiny bit darker. He tried to order his loneliness, to give it a shape so it could fit upon his tongue, but it only slid back and choked him. Then the window came down with a decisive thud, and the light went off again.

He knew he'd be up in her tree forever, and for the first time since taking them, he wanted to return the stars, to make beautiful the sky he would wait beneath.

***

Excerpt of an Interview With a Man Threatening to Blow Up His Local Branch

Tell me again. What are your demands?

A plane to Buenos Aires. A woman for every night I have left. Enough dynamite to blow a hole in the bottom of the sea that sloshes between us all.

You said earlier you wanted to be an inspiration. Can you tell us something inspirational?

Years ago, after the creek flooded and left large puddles all over the soccer field, I saw minnows shimmering there on what had been the grass. No matter how small the puddles became over the coming days, the fish kept looking for a way back to the creek, just 20 feet away.

Did you bring them back to the creek?

I started to, but then I remembered that the creek has reasons to leave its bed. The spurned woman does not return for her toothbrush. She lets the underwear in his hamper become a fond remembrance.

How is this going to end?

With a bang and with a whimper. With a reason to take a shower. It will be as though the loudest band in the world played a single note, unrehearsed.

Before you left for the bank this morning, did you turn off the stereo in your apartment? Did you leave the door unlocked?

No and yes. I wanted there to be a soundtrack playing when they came to search my rooms, and I didn't want them to hurt themselves when breaking down my door.

But you said that your dog is rigged with plastic explosives.

Yes, he is very friendly. They will reach to pet him. They will set off the device.

Why don't you let the children go?

Because they will amplify my message. Because they remind me of minnows.

Is there a way to make you reconsider? To turn back the clock to this morning, before you'd even thought of coming into this bank?

The bank has spent a lifetime moving into my path. Go ask the architect and zoning board why they taunted me like this.

Do you have any last words?

Last words are for those who believe they will not speak again. But already your machines have made me immortal.

What is this yellow button for?

When I press it, an ultrasonic frequency is emitted that attracts moths to this metal plate. When enough of them land, the bomb will explode.

That sounds like something out of a movie about a madman whose genius is for complicated death.

Thank you. I pressed it hours ago. There don't seem to be many moths inside this bank. Luckily I had this other button. It attracts television crews.

Can't you be reasonable?

I'd rather be inspirational. I am a fist full of hidden confetti. I do what your cameras desire.

***

279 Waterloo Street

I could see the dark paint where the number had fallen from her front door. Unfaded I should say. That ghost of a 9 was the only part displaying the door's true and intended red. You can't just touch something like that up. You'd end up with a blotch instead of a 9.

To get the 9 to the exact shade as the rest of the door, you'd have to let it weather — to expose it for years to the blazing noon, to the knuckles of men, to the shit of birds, to the damage done by a decade's worth of breeze.

But even then, the rest of the door would have advanced toward some state of lesser vibrancy. No, you would have to tape up the door — everything but the 9 — and you'd have to hope for the same weather that preceded its disappearance. A whole decade of it. And then the monthly checking, peeling back the tape to see if the door was done.

Left alone, the house would eventually be known as 27 Waterloo Street, instead of 279. Letters would still come for 279 Waterloo Street, of course. But the postman would understand.

You could break down and just paint the whole thing, I suppose. But what a waste of paint — expending it for the sake of a simple 9. Two coats, no doubt. A roll of masking tape. An afternoon. And surely a good shirt ruined from leaning into the paint.

And look — there in the bushes, the glint of her 9 flashing like a wedding band that might as well be at the bottom of the sea. This isn't the kind of place where things climb back to where they belong. Just look around: the basketball held in the deepening weeds, the statue of some saint toppled into the phlox, the little pile of shingle sand at the end of every downspout.

No need to get back out. I gun the car right up the block, over the bridge, and onto the interstate. My plan is to find a different door, and to nail its numbers tight.

***

STARS

He was thinking of the sparkling frost on the trashcan lid as he slammed it back down in the moonlight. He had to slam it because the can was dented and the lid didn't fit right without some force. He was worried about raccoons.

He thought harder. There were other things that had happened, that he had seen, that made him feel like that brief, million-starred constellation that shimmered as he lifted it, leaving two days' worth of apple cores and chicken parts and dirty paper towels to freeze itself into oblivion. This kind of cold kept everything from stinking. He turned and trudged back up to the house, following his footprints in the frosty grass.

There was the pile of down and blue jay feathers he'd found in the woods. There wasn't any blood — every bit of the edible bird had been eaten, taken in, devoured. It looked like a dull supernova against the snowless December brown of the forest floor, as if the bird had rushed into the beyond and left only the smoke of its feathers.

The cold he felt crossing the yard had come from no-where. It was warm only yesterday, no need for a jacket. He remembered the childhood bedroom that overlooked a streetlight, how when they had moved in, he believed the moon was different in that part of the country, that it didn't drift across a window the way it did elsewhere. He figured it out by the end of the week, of course. It took that long for him to disobey his father's order to stay in the bed. And then he saw it was just a streetlamp — a simple light con-nected to a pole, ordinary. He was disappointed. Although he hadn't put it into words until just now, he was vaguely excited, even encouraged, that the sky might be different above that new house.

It seems silly now, but until that house he had never lived with streetlights. They were something he saw in the movies.

And there were the sudden nebulas of fog that drifted off the creeks that ran behind other houses, the deep-space black of an attic, the slow and tailless meteors of the jets above his home — above every home, no matter where he lived.

He was at the back door now. He stopped with his fingers on the handle — listening for raccoons, for the sounds of his children cleaning up their dinner. He felt that he could lift his arms and float up into the stars, that the stars were hidden all around him, that he could see them if he angled his world just so — like a trash can lid beneath the mineral glare of the moon. But no. His father was dead. The world was only cold.

***

WORDS

"Stop putting words in my mouth," she said. She took a long sip of her merlot and eyed him above the rim of her glass. Through the living room window behind her, the traffic was backing up on the rural road that ran before their house — the way it would if a tractor was pulling out of a field at dinner time, or if somebody's dog had been run down.

Not being one to give up easily, he tried to slip in "pimento," "sea salt," "mandolin" and "mauve." She put her glass down on the coffee table, too hard, and a splash of wine leaped over the rim, ran down the stem, and hit the doily, spreading like a bruise. She wasn't taking these words either, and she spit them out as if she'd sipped from a drink with a cigarette floating in it.

"You're pissing me off," she said.

Was she serious? He couldn't tell. He thought she had smiled. He thought it looked dirty. He tried to feed her "surrender" and "dynamite" and "Ferris wheel."

She moved closer. She said, "I told you to stop." Then

she finished her wine and stared into his eyes, leaving the room full of the ambiguity he was used to living with after so many years.

"But I like the sound of them in your mouth, in my ear," he said. "They sound better when you say them. They sound like a plan — like the evening has an X in it that tells me where to dig."

She didn't say anything to that. At the other end of the room, the TV was going through its nightly convulsions, telling them the world was ending as quickly as it could — or as fast as they would let it. It didn't much matter which. She got up and unbuttoned her blouse. She walked down the hall to their bedroom. Was this an invitation, or was it her response to the August air?

Outside the window, the cars were starting to pull away now. The street was clearing the way a river unclogs itself of ice.

He looked down the empty hall. "Say 'triumph,'" he yelled. "Say 'tangerine.'" Nothing came back. Just the road getting darker as the cars drifted off. Just the blackness of the bedroom door half-opened. He picked up the bottle and headed towards her.

"Thirst" was the word he was thinking, but could not bear to say.

***

The Spill

At the train station, he chose the chair beside a coffee spill in the shape of Illinois. His train would arrive in half an hour. He had nothing to read as he waited.

There were other chairs he might have chosen — the station was practically empty. But never in his life had he sat beside somebody else's spill by choice. His foot was only inches away. He checked now and then to see if it was spreading.

Right away he noticed people giving him dirty looks. They assumed it was his mess — and that he had the audacity to continue sitting beside it. The Styrofoam cup rolled slightly from the breeze of their passing feet beside the Illinois-shaped lake of coffee heavily diluted with cream.

Would somebody say something to him? Would he be confronted? He almost wished for it. What a treat for the world to see the slob and his mess connected, to see justice done. It was reason enough for sitting there, for refusing to clean it up.

A woman with a mop appeared. She pushed a pail toward him. It had a wobbling wheel that threatened to send her off-course. He could see already that the water was dirty — the shiniest engagement ring dropped into it would instantly disappear. The woman pinched the water out with the ringer, then let a thousand dampened strings hit the floor with a thud. She swirled it around, erasing Illinois from the linoleum.

The man had loved a woman in Illinois once. He still thought about her — every day at least — sometimes with desire, often with regret. He wondered if he would erase her memory if he could do it as easily as this woman erased Illinois.

The woman with the mop gave him a last and superior look, and pushed the pail toward the other side of the station. Perhaps somebody there had dropped crumbs from a cookie in the shape of Indonesia, where his fiancée — the woman from Illinois — had lost her virginity in a parking lot after necking with a tourist who convinced her, with surprisingly little effort, to try some of the dog that he was eating.

***

The Man Waiting for the Light to Change

It was a windy morning. High up above the buildings of Stamford, he saw a bit of silvery trash as it winked and sailed, higher than birds, higher than chimney smoke, above the buses and trains and the hundreds of cars that had betrayed them to their jobs, that had gotten them there without accident or breakdown or loss of blood. The pigeons huddled on a wire waiting for the sun to hit them. The smell of the Sound, which was likely sparkling and full of tied-up yachts with seagulls scything at the air, drifted through the streets. It was a faint odor, but unquestionably there. Then the light changed, and he hurried in a crowd across the street and into the revolving doors. Like everyone else, he believed his reasoning was sound.

***

Modest Blouses and Flowing Skirts

The woman was late, and he began to worry over the sirens he heard earlier about the time when she would have arrived. He consoled himself by remembering her reputation for always being late, and came to believe these sirens in the distance could have nothing to do with her. They were irrelevant — like an appendix, like the extra fork he was sometimes left with at the end of a restaurant dinner. Still, the sirens had come vaguely from the direction of her arrival. He considered calling to make sure she was okay, and that she hadn't forgotten about their meeting, their date, where after a home-cooked dinner and a romantic comedy and a bottle of merlot, he would try to remove her clothing, for he imagined her body was beautiful beneath her modest blouses and flowing skirts. But if he called, and she *were* on the way, she might try to answer, to dig the phone from her purse while negotiating a snowy curve. His call, he reasoned, might well cause the accident he was trying to prove had never happened. He turned down the heat on the pot of boiling potatoes, and started to arrange the place settings so that they looked even more like the tables in *Fine Cooking*. Later, when she was very late, he walked onto the porch with a whiskey beneath the stars that were always there. As usual, they had nothing to say — not about his future or the wilted salad or the lovely skin he had yet to see beneath her modest blouses and flowing skirts.

***

A Boy Woke Up Beside a Girl

Spiders and wetness. That was the world to which he woke. The grasses and the ground and the leafy wall of the blueberry bushes were covered with webs that had spent the night gathering dew. Every thread was heavy with it, and there was a sense that things might never move again.

The girl who had followed him into the woods was beside him still — beautiful, hungover, curled deeply into his sleeping bag. He wanted her to stay like that forever, but he had to pee.

That's when he saw the river, not thirty feet away. It made no noise because the land was flat. It was dark and red, snaking through the pines like dirty blood. He looked upstream as he relieved himself, trying to understand what was pushing it all his way.

***

Fomite
Burlington, VT

A fomite is a medium capable of transmitting infectious organisms from one individual to another.

"The activity of art is based on the capacity of people to be infected by the feelings of others." Tolstoy, *What Is Art?*

Flight and Other Stories - Jay Boyer

In *Flight and Other Stories*, we're with the fattest woman on earth as she draws her last breaths and her soul ascends toward its final reward. We meet a divorcee who can fly with no more effort than flapping her arms. We follow a middle-aged butler whose love affair with a young woman leads him first to the mysteries of bondage and then to the pleasures of malice. Story by story, we set foot into worlds so strange as to seem all but surreal, yet everything feels familiar, each moment rings true. And that's when we recognize we're in the hands of one of America's truly original talents.

Loisaida - Dan Chodorokoff

Catherine, a young anarchist estranged from her parents and squatting in an abandoned building on New York's Lower East Side, is fighting with her boyfriend and conflicted about her work on an underground newspaper. After learning of a developer's plans to demolish a community garden, Catherine builds an alliance with a group of Puerto Rican community activists. Together they confront the confluence of politics, money, and real estate that rule Manhattan. All the while she learns important lessons from her great-grandmother's life in the Yiddish anarchist movement that flourished on the Lower East Side at the turn of the century. In this coming-of-age story, family saga, and tale of urban politics, Dan Chodorkoff explores the "principle of hope" and examines how memory and imagination inform social change.

Improvisational Arguments - Anna Faktorovich

Improvisational Arguments is written in free verse to capture the essence of modern problems and triumphs. The poems clearly relate short, frequently humorous, and occasionally tragic stories about travels to exotic and unusual places, fantastic realms, abnormal jobs, artistic innovations, political objections, and misadventures with love.

Fomite
Burlington, VT

Loosestrife - Greg Delanty
This book is a chronicle of complicity in our modern lives, a witnessing of war and the destruction of our planet. It is also an attempt to adjust the more destructive blueprint myths of our society. Often our cultural memory tells us to keep quiet about the aspects that are most challenging to our ethics, to forget the violations we feel and tremors that keep us distant and numb.

Carts and Other Stories - Zdravka Evtimova
Roots and wings are the key words that best describe the short story collection *Carts and Other Stories*, by Zdravka Evtimova. The book is emotionally multilayered and memorable because of its internal power, vitality and ability to touch both your heart and your mind. Within its pages, the reader discovers new perspectives and true wealth, and learns to see the world with different eyes. The collection lives on the borders of different cultures. *Carts and Other Stories* will take the reader to wild and powerful Bulgarian mountains, to silver rains in Brussels, to German quiet winter streets, and to wind-bitten crags in Afghanistan. This book lives for those seeking to discover the beauty of the world around them, and will have them appreciating what they have—and perhaps what they have lost as well.

The Listener Aspires to the Condition of Music - Barry Goldensohn
"I know of no other selected poems that selects on one theme, but this one does, charting Goldensohn's career-long attraction to music's performance, consolations and its august, thrilling, scary and clownish charms. Does all art aspire to the condition of music as Pater claimed, exhaling in a swoon toward that one class act? Goldensohn is more aware than the late 19th century of the overtones of such breathing: his poems thoroughly round out those overtones in a poet's lifetime of listening." John Peck, poet, editor, Fellow of the American Academy of Rome

Raven or Crow - Joshua Amses
Marlowe has recently moved back home to Vermont after flunking his first term at a private college in the Midwest, when his sort-of girlfriend, Eleanor, goes missing. The circumstances surrounding Eleanor's disappearance stand to reveal more about Marlowe than he is willing to allow. Rather than report her missing, he resolves to find Eleanor himself. *Raven or Crow* is the story of mistakes rooted in the ambivalence of being young and without direction.

Fomite
Burlington, VT

The Co-Conspirator's Tale - Ron Jacobs

There's a place where love and mistrust are never at peace; where duplicity and deceit are the universal currency. *The Co-Conspirator's Tale* takes place within this nebulous firmament. There are crimes committed by the police in the name of the law. Excess in the name of revolution. The combination leaves death in its wake and the survivors struggling to find justice in a San Francisco Bay Area noir by the author of the underground classic *The Way the Wind Blew: A History of the Weather Underground.*

Short Order Frame Up - Ron Jacobs

1975. America has lost its war in Vietnam and Cambodia. Racially tinged riots are tearing the city of Boston apart. The politics and counterculture of the 1960s are disintegrating into nothing more than sex, drugs, and rock and roll. The Boston Red Sox are on one of their improbable runs toward a postseason appearance. In a suburban town in Maryland, a young couple are murdered and another young man is accused. The couple are white and the accused is black. It is up to his friends and family to prove he is innocent. This is a story of suburban ennui, race, murder, and injustice. Religion and politics, liberal lawyers and racist cops. In *Short Order Frame Up*, Ron Jacobs has written a piece of crime fiction that exposes the wound that is US racism. Two cultures existing side by side and across generations--a river very few dare to cross. His characters work and live with and next to each other, often unaware of each other's real life. When the murder occurs, however, those people that care about the man charged must cross that river and meet somewhere in between in order to free him from (what is to them) an obvious miscarriage of justice.

All the Sinners Saints - Ron Jacobs

A young draftee named Victor Willard goes AWOL in Germany after an altercation with a commanding officer. Porgy is an African-American GI involved with the international Black Panthers and German radicals. Victor and a female radical named Ana fall in love. They move into Ana's room in a squatted building near the US base in Frankfurt. The international campaign to free Black revolutionary Angela Davis is coming to Frankfurt. Porgy and Ana are key organizers and Victor spends his days and nights selling and smoking hashish, while becoming addicted to heroin. Police and narcotics agents are keeping tabs on them all. Politics, love, and drugs. Truths, lies, and rock and roll. *All the Sinners Saints* is a story of people seeking redemption in a world awash in sin.

Fomite
Burlington, VT

When You Remember Deir Yassin - R. L. Green
When You Remember Deir Yassin is a collection of poems by R. L. Green, an American Jewish writer, on the subject of the occupation and destruction of Palestine. Green comments: "Outspoken Jewish critics of Israeli crimes against humanity have, strangely, been called 'anti-Semitic' as well as the hilariously illogical epithet 'self-hating Jews.' As a Jewish critic of the Israeli government, I have come to accept these accusations as a stamp of approval and a badge of honor, signifying my own fealty to a central element of Jewish identity and ethics: one must be a lover of truth and a friend to the oppressed, and stand with the victims of tyranny, not with the tyrants, despite tribal loyalty or self-advancement. These poems were written as expressions of outrage, and of grief, and to encourage my sisters and brothers of every cultural or national grouping to speak out against injustice, to try to save Palestine, and in so doing, to reclaim for myself my own place as part of the Jewish people." Poems in the original English are accompanied by Arabic translations.

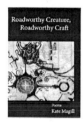

Roadworthy Creature, Roadworthy Craft - Kate Magill
Words fail but the voice struggles on. The culmination of a decade's worth of performance poetry, *Roadworthy Creature, Roadworthy Craft* is Kate Magill's first full-length publication. In lines that are sinewy yet delicate, Magill's poems explore the terrain where idea and action meet, where bodies and words commingle to form a strange new flesh, a breathing text, an "I" that spirals outward from itself.

Zinsky the Obscure - Ilan Mochari
"If your childhood is brutal, your adulthood becomes a daily attempt to recover: a quest for ecstasy and stability in recompense for their early absence." So states the 30-year-old Ariel Zinsky, whose bachelor-like lifestyle belies the torturous youth he is still coming to grips with. As a boy, he struggles with the beatings themselves; as a grownup, he struggles with the world's indifference to them. *Zinsky the Obscure* is his life story, a humorous chronicle of his search for a redemptive ecstasy through sex, an entrepreneurial sports obsession, and finally, the cathartic exercise of writing it all down. Fervently recounting both the comic delights and the frightening horrors of a life in which he feels—always—that he is not like all the rest, Zinsky survives the worst and relishes the best with idiosyncratic style, as his heartbreak turns into self-awareness and his suicidal ideation into self-regard. A vivid evocation of the all-consuming nature of lust and ambition—and the forces that drive them.

Fomite
Burlington, VT

The Derivation of Cowboys & Indians - Joseph D. Reich

The Derivation of Cowboys & Indians represents a profound journey, a breakdown of the American Dream from a social, cultural, historical, and spiritual point of view. Reich examines in concise detail the loss of the collective unconscious, commenting on our contemporary postmodern culture with its self-interested excesses, on where and how things all go wrong, and how social/ political practice rarely meets its original proclamations and promises. Reich's surreal and self-effacing satire brings this troubling message home. *The Derivation of Cowboys & Indians* is a desperate search and struggle for America's literal, symbolic, and spiritual home.

Kasper Planet: Comix and Tragix - Peter Schumann

The British call him Punch; the Italians, Pulchinella; the Russians, Petruchka; the Native Americans, Coyote. These are the figures we may know. But every culture that worships authority will breed a Punch-like, anti-authoritarian resister. Yin and yang—it has to happen. The Germans call him Kasper. Truth-telling and serious pranking are dangerous professions when going up against power. Bradley Manning sits naked in solitary; Julian Assange is pursued by Interpol, Obama's Department of Justice, and Amazon.com. But—in contrast to merely human faces— masks and theater can often slip through the bars. Consider our American Kaspers: Charlie Chaplin, Woody Guthrie, Abby Hoffman, the Yes Men—theater people all, utilizing various forms to seed critique. Their profiles and tactics have evolved along with those of their enemies. Who are the bad guys that call forth the Kaspers? Over the last half century, with his Bread & Puppet Theater, Peter Schumann has been tireless in naming them, excoriating them with Kasperdom....

from Marc Estrin's Foreword to Planet Kasper

Views Cost Extra - L.E. Smith

Views that inspire, that calm, or that terrify—all come at some cost to the viewer. In *Views Cost Extra* you will find a New Jersey high school preppy who wants to inhabit the "perfect" cowboy movie, a rural mailman disgusted with the residents of his town who wants to live with the penguins, an ailing screen-writer who strikes a deal with Johnny Cash to reverse an old man's failures, an old man who ponders a young man's suicide attempt, a one-armed blind blues singer who wants to reunite with the car that took her arm on the assembly line— and more. These stories suggest that we must pay something to live even ordinary lives.

Fomite
Burlington, VT

The Empty Notebook Interrogates Itself - Susan Thomas

The Empty Notebook began its life as a very literal metaphor for a few weeks of what the poet thought was writer's block, but was really the struggle of an eccentric persona to take over her working life. It won. And for the next three years everything she wrote came to her in the voice of the Empty Notebook, who, as the notebook began to fill itself, became rather opinionated, changed gender, alternately acted as bully and victim, had many bizarre adventures in exotic locales, and developed a somewhat politically incorrect attitude. It then began to steal the voices and forms of other poets and tried to immortalize itself in various poetry reviews. It is now thrilled to collect itself in one slim volume.

My God, What Have We Done? - Susan Weiss

In a world afflicted with war, toxicity, and hunger, does what we do in our private lives really matter? Fifty years after the creation of the atomic bomb at Los Alamos, newlyweds Pauline and Clifford visit that once-secret city on their honeymoon, compelled by Pauline's fascination with Oppenheimer, the soulful scientist. The two stories emerging from this visit reverberate back and forth between the loneliness of a new mother at home in Boston and the isolation of an entire community dedicated to the development of the bomb. While Pauline struggles with unforeseen challenges of family life, Oppenheimer and his crew reckon with forces beyond all imagining. Finally the years of frantic research on the bomb culminate in a stunning test explosion that echoes a rupture in the couple's marriage. Against the backdrop of a civilization that's out of control, Pauline begins to understand the complex, potentially explosive physics of personal relationships. At once funny and dead serious, *My God, What Have We Done?* sifts through the ruins left by the bomb in search of a more worthy human achievement.

Entanglements - Tony Magistrale

A poet and a painter may employ different mediums to express the same snow-blown afternoon in January, but sometimes they find a way to capture the moment in such a way that their respective visions still manage to stir a reverberation, a connection. In part, that's what *Entanglements* seeks to do. Not so much for the poems and paintings to speak directly to one another, but for them to stir points of similarity.

Fomite
Burlington, VT

As It Is On Earth - Peter M. Wheelwright
Four centuries after the Reformation Pilgrims sailed up the down-flowing watersheds of New England, Taylor Thatcher, irreverent scion of a fallen family of Maine Puritans, is still caught in the turbulence. In his errant attempts to escape from history, the young college professor is further unsettled by his growing attraction to Israeli student Miryam Bluehm as he is swept by Time through the "family thing"—from the tangled genetic and religious history of his New England parents to the redemptive birthday secret of Esther Fleur Noire Bishop, the Cajun-Passamaquoddy woman who raised him and his younger half-cousin/half-brother, Bingham. The landscapes, rivers, and tidal estuaries of Old New England and the Mayan Yucatan are also casualties of history in Thatcher's story of Deep Time and re-discovery of family on Columbus Day at a high-stakes gambling casino, rising in resurrection over the starlit bones of a once-vanquished Pequot Indian tribe.

Suite for Three Voices - Derek Furr
Suite for Three Voices is a dance of prose genres, teeming with intense human life in all its humor and sorrow. A son uncovers the horrors of his father's wartime experience, a hitchhiker in a muumuu guards a mysterious parcel, a young man foresees his brother's brush with death on September 11. A Victorian poetess encounters space aliens and digital archives, a runner hears the voice of a dead friend in the song of an indigo bunting, a teacher seeks wisdom from his students' errors and Neil Young. By frozen waterfalls and neglected graveyards, along highways at noon and rivers at dusk, in the sound of bluegrass, Beethoven, and Emily Dickinson, the essays and fiction in this collection offer moments of vision.

The Good Muslim of Jackson Heights - Jaysinh Birjépatil
Jackson Heights in this book is a fictional locale with common features assembled from immigrant-friendly neighborhoods around the world where hardworking honest-to-goodness traders from the Indian subcontinent rub shoulders with ruthless entrepreneurs, reclusive antique-dealers, homeless nobodies, merchant-princes, lawyers, doctors, and IT specialists. But as Siraj and Shabnam, urbane newcomers fleeing religious persecution in their homeland, discover, there is no escape from the past. Weaving together the personal and the political. The Good Muslim of Jackson Heights is an ambiguous elegy to a utopian ideal set free from all prejudice.

Fomite
Burlington, VT

Travers' Inferno - *L.E. Smith*

In the 1970's, churches began to burn in Burlington, Vermont. If it was arson, no one or no reason could be found to blame. This book suggests arson, but makes no claim to historical realism. It claims, instead, to capture the dizzying 70's zeitgeist of aggressive utopian movements, distrust in authority, escapist alternative lifestyles, and a bewildered society of onlookers. In the tradition of John Gardner's *Sunlight Dialogues*, the characters of *Travers' Inferno* are colorful and damaged, sometimes comical, sometimes tragic, looking for meaning through desperate acts. Travers Jones, the protagonist, is grounded in the transcendent—philosophy, epilepsy, arson as purification—and mystified by the opposite sex, haunted by an absent father and directed by an uncle with a grudge. He is seduced by a professor's wife and chased by an endearing if ineffective sergeant of police. There are secessionist Quebecois involved in these church burns who are murdering as well as pilfering and burning. There are changing alliances, violent deaths, lovemaking, and a belligerent cat.

Still Time - Michael Cocchiarale

Still Time is a collection of twenty-five short and shorter stories exploring tensions that arise in a variety of contemporary relationships: a young boy must deal with the wrath of his out-of-work father; a woman runs into a man twenty years after an awkward sexual encounter; a wife, unable to conceive, imagines her own murder, as well as the reaction of her emotionally distant husband; a soon-to-be-tenured English professor tries to come to terms with her husband's shocking return to the religion of his youth; an assembly line worker, married for thirty years, discovers the surprising secret life of his recently hospitalized wife. Whether a few hundred or a few thousand words, these and other stories in the collection depict characters at moments of deep crisis. Some feel powerless, overwhelmed—unable to do much to change the course of their lives. Others rise to the occasion and, for better or for worse, say or do the thing that might transform them for good. Even in stories with the most troubling of endings, there remains the possibility of redemption. For each of the characters, there is still time.

Screwed – Stephen Goldberg

Screwed is a collection of five plays by Stephen Goldberg, who has written over twenty-five produced plays and is co-founder of the Off Center or the Dramatic Arts in Burlington, Vermont.

Fomite
Burlington, VT

Signed Confessions - *Tom Walker*
Guilt and a desperate need to repent drive the antiheroes in Tom Walker's dark (and often darkly funny) stories: a gullible journalist falls for the 40-year-old stripper he profiles in a magazine, a faithless husband abandons his family and joins a support group for lost souls, a merciless prosecuting attorney grapples with the suicide of his gay son, an aging misanthrope must make amends to five former victims, an egoistic naval hero is haunted by apparitions of his dead wife and a mysterious little girl. The seven tales in *Signed Confessions* measure how far guilty men will go to obtain a forgiveness no one can grant but themselves.

The Housing Market - *Joseph D. Reich*
In Joseph Reich's most recent social and cultural, contemporary satire
of suburbia entitled, "The Housing market: a comfortable place to jump
off the end of the world," the author addresses the absurd, postmodern
elements of what it means, or for that matter not, to try and cope and
function, and survive and thrive, or live and die in the repetitive and existential, futile and self-destructive, homogenized, monochromatic landscape of a brutal and bland, collective unconscious, which can spiritually result in a gradual wasting away and erosion of the senses or conflict and crisis of a desperate, disproportionate 'situational depression,' triggering and leading the narrator to feel constantly abandoned and stranded, more concretely or proverbially spoken, "the eternal stranger," where when caught between the fight or flight psychological phenomena, naturally repels him and causes him to flee and return without him even knowing it into the wild, while by sudden circumstance and coincidence discovers it surrounds the illusory-like circumference of these selfsame Monopoly board cul-de-sacs and dead ends. Most specifically, what can happen to a solitary, thoughtful, and independent thinker when being stagnated in the triangulation of a cookie-cutter, oppressive culture of a homeowner's association; a memoir all written in critical and didactic, poetic stanzas and passages, and out of desperation, when freedom and control get taken, what he is forced to do in the illusion of 'free will and volition,' something like the derivative art of a smart and ironic and social and cultural satire.

Fomite
Burlington, VT

Love's Labours - Jack Pulaski

In the four stories and two novellas that comprise *Love's Labors* the protagonists, Ben and Laura, discover in their fervid romance and long marriage their interlocking fates, and the histories that preceded their births. They also learned something of the paradox between love and all the things it brings to its beneficiaries: bliss, disaster, duty, tragedy, comedy, the grotesque, and tenderness.

Ben and Laura's story is also the particularly American tale of immigration to a new world. Laura's story begins in Puerto Rico, and Ben's lineage is Russian-Jewish. They meet in City College of New York, a place at least analogous to a melting pot. Laura struggles to rescue her brother from gang life and heroin. She is mother to her younger sister; their mother Consuelo is the financial mainstay of the family and consumed by work. Despite filial obligations, Laura aspires to be a serious painter. Ben writes, cares for, and is caught up in the misadventures and surreal stories of his younger schizophrenic brother. Laura is also a story teller as powerful and enchanting as Scheherazade. Ben struggles to survive such riches, and he and Laura endure.

Meanwell - *Janice Miller Potter*

Meanwell is a twenty-four-poem sequence in which a female servant searches for identity and meaning in the shadow of her mistress, poet Anne Bradstreet. Although Meanwell herself is a fiction, someone like her could easily have existed among Bradstreet's known but unnamed domestic servants. Through Meanwell's eyes, Bradstreet emerges as a human figure during the Great Migration of the 1600s, a period in which the Massachusetts Bay Colony was fraught with physical and political dangers. Through Meanwell, the feelings of women, silenced during the midwife Anne Hutchinson's fiery trial before the Puritan ministers, are finally acknowledged. In effect, the poems are about the making of an American rebel. Through her conflicted conscience, we witness Meanwell's transformation from a powerless English waif to a mythic American who ultimately chooses wilderness over the civilization she has experienced.

Visiting Hours - *Jennifer Anne Moses*

Visiting Hours, a novel-in-stories, explores the lives of people not normally met on the page——AIDS patients and those who care for them. Set in Baton Rouge, Louisiana, and written with large and frequent dollops of humor, the book is a profound meditation on faith and love in the face of illness and poverty.

Fomite
Burlington, VT

Four-Way Stop - Sherry Olson

If *Thank You* were the only prayer, as Meister Eckhart has suggested, it would be enough, and Sherry Olson's poetry, in her second book, *Four-Way Stop*, would be one. Radical attention, deep love, and dedication to kindness illuminate these poems and the stories she tells us, which are drawn from her own life: with family, with friends, and wherever she travels, with strangers – who to Olson, never are strangers, but kin. Even at the difficult intersections, as in the title poem, *Four-Way Stop*, Olson experiences – and offers – hope, showing us how, *completely unsupervised*, people take turns, with *kindness waving each other on*. Olson writes, knowing that (to quote Czeslaw Milosz) *What surrounds us, here and now, is not guaranteed*. To this world, with her poems, Olson brings – and teaches – attention, generosity, compassion, and appreciative joy. —Carol Henrikson

Body of Work - Andrei Guruianu

Throughout thirteen stories, Body of Work chronicles the physical and emotional toll of characters consumed by the all-too-human need for a connection. Their world is achingly common — beauty and regret, obsession and self-doubt, the seductive charm of loneliness. Often fragmented, whimsical, always on the verge of melancholy, the collection is a sepia-toned portrait of nostalgia — each story like an artifact of our impermanence, an embrace of all that we have lost, of all that we might lose and love again someday.

Dons of Time - Greg Guma

"Wherever you look…there you are." The next media breakthrough has just happened. They call it Remote Viewing and Tonio Wolfe is at the center of the storm. But the research underway at TELPORT's off-the-books lab is even more radical -- opening a window not only to remote places but completely different times. Now unsolved mysteries are colliding with cutting edge science and altered states of consciousness in a world of corporate gangsters, infamous crimes and top-secret experiments. Based on eyewitness accounts, suppressed documents and the lives of world-changers like Nikola Tesla, Annie Besant and Jack the Ripper, Dons of Time is a speculative adventure, a glimpse of an alternative future and a quantum leap to Gilded Age London at the tipping point of invention, revolution and murder.

Fomite
Burlington, VT

Alfabestiario
AlphaBetaBestiario - Antonello Borra
Animals have always understood that mankind is not fully at home in the world. Bestiaries, hoping to teach, send out warnings. This one, of course, aims at doing the same.

Writing a review on Amazon, Good Reads, Shelfari, Library Thing or other social media sites for readers will help the progress of independent publishing. To submit a review, go to the book page on any of the sites and follow the links for reviews. Books from independent presses rely on reader to reader communications.

CPSIA information can be obtained
at www.ICGtesting.com
Printed in the USA
LVOW12s2343070916
503690LV00001B/2/P